"Come back to Holyoake with me, Ginny."

Fear shot through her eyes. "And bring trouble home? No way."

At her words, Ben felt all the anger that had built up inside him when he'd argued with Ginny the day before begin to drain away. Did she think she had to stay away from her family in order to protect them from whoever was after her? Now her stubborn refusal to return home made perfect sense. But he still didn't like it.

"Ginny, you can't face these threats alone."

"Why not? I've made it this far, haven't I?"

Ben leaned back and regarded her tear-streaked face, from her disheveled red hair to a soot smudge on her freckled chin. So this was the real Ginger McAlister, the fearless aviatrix he'd revered for so long. He felt a tug on his heart that was unlike anything he'd ever known in all his thirty-eight years of bachelorhood.

And then he pulled her tight against his shoulder again. "I'm going to keep you safe, Ginny McCutcheon."

Books by Rachelle McCalla

Love Inspired Suspense

Survival Instinct
Troubled Waters
Out on a Limb
Danger on Her Doorstep
Dead Reckoning

RACHELLE McCALLA

is a mild-mannered housewife, and the toughest she ever has to get is when she's trying to keep her four kids quiet in church. Though she often gets in over her head, as her characters do, and has to find a way out, her adventures have more to do with sorting out the carpool and providing food for the potluck. She's never been arrested, gotten in a fistfight or been shot at. And she'd like to keep it that way! For recipes, fun background notes on the places and characters in this book and more information on forthcoming titles, visit www.rachellemccalla.com.

DEAD RECKONING

RACHELLE McCALLA

Love Inspired

Recycling programs for this product may not exist in your area.

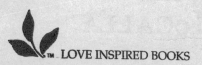

™ LOVE INSPIRED BOOKS

ISBN-13: 978-0-373-44450-2

DEAD RECKONING

Copyright © 2011 by Rachelle McCalla

www.LoveInspiredBooks.com

Printed in U.S.A.

Dedication

In memory of Chandy Clanton, stunt pilot
and aerobatics flier who died while flying her
Edge 540 aircraft in preparation for the
Wingnuts Flying Circus in Tarkio, Missouri,
on July 10, 2009. She was thirty-six years old
and left behind two young sons. My family was
privileged to watch her fly at the Clarinda
Air Show a few weeks prior to her death.
Chandy was and always will be an inspiration.

Acknowledgments

Tremendous thanks go out to all those individuals
who provided invaluable assistance to me while
writing this book. Thank you Mark Vinton and
Rich Murphy for all your technical expertise on
small aircraft and radio communication. Thanks
also to my early readers, especially Brittany
Richter, Sharon Dunn and Sandra Robbins, for
helping me make this crazy story make sense!
Special thanks to Ray and the kids, for your love
for pizza and PB and J. As always, thank you,
Emily Rodmell, editor extraordinaire, for your
patience and vision. And eternal thanks to my Lord
and Savior Jesus Christ, for everything.

What do you think? If a man owns a hundred sheep, and one of them wanders away, will he not leave the ninety-nine on the hills and go to look for the one that wandered off? And if he finds it, I tell you the truth, he is happier about that one sheep than about the ninety-nine that did not wander off.

In the same way your Father in heaven is not willing that any of these little ones should be lost.

—*Matthew* 18:12–24

ONE

She didn't have time to blink. Ginny McCutcheon flew her plane low over the wide-open high plains of eastern Wyoming and was just pulling out of a loop-the-loop when she spotted another plane bearing down on her. Her evasive maneuver was pure reflex—she snapped into a vertical bank, swerving off to the right and trying to pull up, though her downward-pointed wing sliced so close to the ground that the tops of the prairie grasses slapped against its tip.

That was way too close for comfort.

Flipping upside down as she came around, Ginny twisted her head for some sign of where the other plane had gone, and spotted it in a hairpin arc behind her. What kind of maniac was flying that thing, anyway? And what was he doing in her air zone? The Dare Divas Barnstorming Troupe kept to a strict practice schedule; no one was supposed to be in her airspace.

Ginny's heart beat hard, and she felt the same painful squeeze of fright she'd felt the last time she'd nearly lost her life in the air. There had been too many suspicious incidents lately, too many close calls. First Kristy Keller's accident, then the gunshots that had narrowly missed Ginny, not to mention irregular engine troubles that had plagued the Divas' planes. If she was the paranoid type, she might have thought someone was targeting her troupe.

Rather than risk an in-air collision, Ginny found a relatively level spot and brought the plane down to land. Her wheels didn't like the tall prairie grasses, but she wasn't about to risk crossing the flight path of the other plane by heading toward the landing strip five miles west. She struggled to inhale against the fear that clenched at her heart. If flying didn't kill her, the stress would.

As her snub-nosed stunt plane quickly shed its momentum, Ginny caught sight of the other plane again, landing on the same stretch of level ground—headed straight for her again! The other pilot was apparently trying to get out of her way, but he'd picked the same stretch of ground to land on that she had.

With no room to try to take off with the other plane in her way, Ginny threw herself into the brake, gritting her teeth as her plane finally came to a stop nose to nose with the other plane. Her feet hit the ground a moment later.

"What do you think you're doing?" she screamed as the door opened on the other aircraft. That plane clearly didn't belong to the barnstorming fleet. She'd never seen it before. Probably another reporter, maybe a news crew. They'd been everywhere since Kristy's accident, hounding the rest of the Dare Divas and looking for answers about what had happened. Ginny only wished she had answers to give them—especially since Kristy's accident had occurred when she'd been flying Ginny's plane, in Ginny's act. Guilt toyed with her fear-clenched heart. It should have been Ginny at the controls that day.

Right now, she was fixing to give the imbecile inside a piece of her mind for flying so dangerously close during her practice session. But the moment she saw the size of the boots that came through the door of the plane, Ginny realized it wasn't some sheepish, small-framed news-hound.

Two trunk-like legs followed, landing solidly in the prairie grass as a trim waist and broad shoulders ducked under the wing to approach her.

For one terrified moment, Ginny was eight years old again, running out of the house intending to scare off the neighbor's milk cow that had gotten into the garden for the fifteenth time, only to have the bovine beast turn around and point its horns at her. It hadn't been a cow that day. It had been a bull.

Fortunately, the bull had been more interested in her mother's sweet corn than in chasing Ginny, and she'd gotten away with nothing more than a skinned knee as she'd tripped over herself trying to run back inside.

But she could tell she wouldn't be so lucky today. If his determined stride was any indication, this pilot looked ready to lock horns and fight.

"What am *I* doing? What are *you* doing?" he growled. "Do you realize you almost got us both killed? Haven't you ever heard of flying in a straight line?"

Ginny's anger flared. No way was she going to stand there and let this giant of a man bully her. *"Me?"* she shrieked. "I was assigned to this practice zone. This is Dare Diva airspace, and you have no legal right to be here."

"Dare Diva airspace?" The pilot came to a stop less than two feet from her, towering over her, which was saying something, since at five foot ten she was taller than many men. This guy was big.

"The barnstorming flying troupe." She took a step back, peeling off her flying helmet so she could see him better. She shook out her long, red hair as it tumbled free of her helmet in a move that had become her signature on the stunt flying circuit—though anyone who'd ever tried to stuff thick, waist-length hair into a flying helmet would tell you there was no other way to free it.

Though she hadn't meant to make any sort of impression on the other pilot, she caught a second's satisfaction as his jaw dropped and he watched, dumbfounded, as her hair fell free.

Her feeling of satisfaction was immediately erased by the next words to fall from his lips.

"Little Ginny McCutcheon."

Ginny's blood froze. How did he know her name—her real name? Her flying moniker was Ginger McAlister, and that was all anybody outside her hometown of Holyoake, Iowa, was supposed to know her by. "There's no Ginny McCutcheon here," she corrected him quickly.

But his eyes had turned up at the corners and he looked far too pleased with himself. "Excuse me, then. I suppose you're Ginger McAlister?"

An icy chill trickled through her veins. How did this man know *both* her names? Nobody in Wyoming was supposed to know her Iowa identity. And the only person in Iowa who knew the name she flew under was her older brother, Cutch, and he'd been sworn to secrecy. Ginny thought about the stray gunshots that had narrowly missed hitting her twice in the past two weeks, as well as Kristy Keller's accident, which had happened while her fellow pilot had been flying *her* plane.

Too many near misses.

Too many unanswered questions.

"Who are you?" Ginny glared up at the mysterious man who'd so narrowly avoided colliding with her in midair.

"Funny you should ask that." He peeled back his helmet, revealing a strong-featured face that struck Ginny first as being handsome, and then, as she struggled to think past that fact, as oddly familiar. But not one she'd seen any time lately.

"Ben McAlister." The man introduced himself and extended a beefy hand her way.

His hand hovered between them for a moment while Ginny sorted out what this new revelation meant. Ben McAlister was from Holyoake, Iowa. She'd heard all about him when he'd joined the Air Force right out of high school, going on to become a hero fighter pilot back when she was still too young to follow in his footsteps. He was the reason she'd chosen the McAlister name to fly under—because he was the greatest pilot she'd ever known who wasn't a McCutcheon. And there was no way she was going to fly under her own name.

Swallowing hard, she shifted her helmet to her hip and took the big man's hand. She'd seen this guy march in Fourth of July parades many times, but had never come so close to him. His hand closed gently over hers and she felt her pain-clenched heart nearly stop.

Wow. Ben McAlister was shaking her hand.

What on earth was he doing in Wyoming?

"What are you doing here?" She summoned up some of the fire that had gone out when he'd taken her hand.

His hazel eyes looked a little too pleased as he smiled down at her. "Your brother sent me to bring you home."

"Whoa." Ginny pulled her hand away from his and took a couple of steps back toward her plane. "No deal."

His smile disappeared. "His wedding is two weeks from tomorrow. He wants you to be there." He had a deep, rumbling voice that reminded her of a plane engine purring smoothly with a steady tailwind.

"I'll be there," Ginny nearly shouted as the brisk Wyoming airstream whistled through the space between them as she backed away, feeling the need to escape, to put distance between herself and anything having to do with her hometown. "It's not for over two weeks."

"But there's a shower, parties, the rehearsal." Ben's long legs brought him closer to her in a single stride. "And dress fittings."

"It's a dress. How well does it have to fit?" She shook her head, throwing off his arguments like a dog shaking off water. "I have obligations here. I'll be there in time for the rehearsal, okay?"

"Ginny." Ben's voice dipped an octave and he bent his face closer to hers. "This is important to your brother and his new wife—"

But his words were cut off as the alarm on Ginny's watch began to bleat. "My training time is up," she informed Ben flatly, glad to have an excuse to end a conversation she really didn't want to be having anyway. "If we're not out of this training zone in ten minutes, you'll have another stunt pilot to tangle with."

"I can follow you in," Ben volunteered.

Ginny hadn't figured she'd lose him very easily. "Fine. Just don't crowd me."

"I'll try not to." He headed back toward his plane, pausing before he climbed into the cockpit. "By the way, that was some mighty fine flying you did up there. I thought for a second we were both done for."

Ginny tried her best not to smile, but the corners of her mouth angled up in spite of her efforts. "You, too," she said finally, and watched him climb aboard before heading back to her own plane and beginning the laborious process of stuffing her hair back inside her flight helmet in an orderly fashion.

By the time she had her head back up, Ben had gotten his plane turned around and was artfully executing a skilled takeoff from the less-than-optimum surface of the grassy plain. With his plane now out of her way, she could take off, and he could circle around and follow her in.

She took a deep breath, glad to have him gone, for the moment, at least. But even then, the pain that squeezed her chest didn't go away. The doctors she'd seen had chalked up the ever-present pain to stress, and told her to find a less frightening occupation, which she wasn't about to do. She loved stunt flying and the sense of freedom she felt when she was in the sky. Nothing would ever change that.

After making sure Ben had flown wide and clear of her intended takeoff route, Ginny got her plane into the air and headed back to the Dare Diva training headquarters, thoughts buzzing through her mind. If Ben thought he was going to get her to turn her back on her responsibilities with the Dare Divas and go back to her oppressive hometown, he was mistaken. Her training schedule had suffered enough interruptions with all the recent incidents.

As the wheels of her stunt plane touched down on the hardened soil of the Wyoming airfield, she felt her anger at Ben's interruption recede as fear clenched its fingers tighter around her heart. Maybe she was just paranoid after everything that had happened lately, but it was almost as though she could smell danger on the wind. Years before, when her grandfather had first taught her how to fly, he'd always said landing was the most dangerous part of flying. But lately Ginny had learned to expect trouble at any time.

As she taxied the small plane toward the largest hangar and through the wide-open door, she saw with a sinking feeling that the light was still out near the back, leaving the far corner of the hangar in shadowy darkness. Ginny didn't like it, but she forced herself to take slow, steady breaths as she parked her plane in the corner where it belonged, hoping to exit quickly and leave the darkness behind.

But as she jumped down from the plane, she heard a voice call. "Ginger?"

Ginger McAlister—her flying name. Since Ben had kept his promise to stay well behind her when she landed, she knew it wasn't him. He was likely still in the air. It was probably a fan, or maybe one of those nosy reporters who'd been everywhere since Kristy's accident. It seemed the Dare Divas brought trouble with them wherever they went lately.

"Yes?" She peered into the shadows, her eyes still sun-blinded from the bright sky she'd been flying in. A red orb glowed hot as someone in the darkness sucked in on a cigarette. Ginny picked up the scent over the smell of fuel and oil.

"You're not allowed to smoke in the hangar," she informed the shadowy figure. "It's a safety hazard—against the rules."

"Rules were made to be broken," the gravelly voice said as the glowing cigarette fell to the floor. He crushed it with his boot as he advanced toward her.

Not good. Ginny loved her fans, but creepy guys who blatantly disregarded the rules were another thing entirely.

"I just want your autograph." The man's tobacco breath stung her nose as he placed his hand on her arm, his grip uncomfortably tight.

Ginny felt pain stab through her heart as a sense of panic rose inside her. They were in a dark corner of the hangar and from what she'd seen, the rest of the Dare Divas and their crew were outside or on the far side of the hangar where plane engines whirred, their high-pitched hums more than enough to drown out her voice if she cried out, even if she screamed.

Oh, so very not good.

"Just let me get a pen," Ginny said, trying to sound unconcerned as she took a step toward the light, and safety.

The hand tightened around her arm. Ouch. That was going to leave a bruise.

A silver shaft appeared.

"I've already got one."

"How convenient," Ginny raised her voice a little, hoping to catch someone's attention, trying to turn around so she could at least see if anyone was within hearing distance. But the man completely blocked her view with his big, sweaty body, and his grip on her arm held her securely in place.

Ginny's heart hammered hard inside her. She was used to keeping a cool head under stress, but that was when she was flying. Here on the ground she felt a lot more vulnerable.

"And where would you like me to sign?" She could only hope he'd leave her alone once she'd fulfilled his request.

"My shoulder," he sneered. "Then I can get it tattooed."

Ginny swallowed. So very creepy. "Pen?" she asked, unable to trust her voice to speak more than one word without shaking. Something told her she didn't want to let on to this guy just how much he frightened her. If she'd thought God would answer, she might have even started praying.

The stranger pressed the cold metal into her hand.

"Where exactly do you want it?" She wished he'd let go of her and step away enough to permit her to make a break for it. Another engine started up near the entrance to the hangar—the next shift of planes preparing for their practice times. Nobody was going to hear her over that noise.

"Let's take it on the road," he said suddenly, wrapping his other arm around her and picking her up as he headed for the rear exit.

No! Ginny tried to stomp his foot, but he held her too high. She tried to cry out, but the man's sweaty hand clamped over her mouth. She thrashed and struggled as he made his way too quickly toward the door.

She couldn't let him get through the exit! There was nothing back there but a stand of trees and an old road that led into the Wyoming wilderness. She had a feeling if she let him carry her off, she'd never be seen again. Not alive, anyway.

He let go of her mouth just long enough to reach for the doorknob.

Ginny kicked out, screaming. "Help! Help me!" Panic infused her voice, but the sound of plane engines echoed even louder. "Let me *go!*"

The man got the door partway open, and a slice of light streamed in.

"Help me! Help!" Ginny screamed with all her might just before the man's grimy hand covered her mouth again.

Suddenly Ginny heard a hollow thump as a shudder stilled the man and his grip relaxed. She twisted away, spiraling backward until her back hit the cold metal slab of the door. She looked up in time to see a large figure draw back a mighty fist, which he leveled at her attacker's jaw.

The sweaty head snapped back, and the guy went down.

Across the hangar, three planes exited toward the runways, taking the noise of their engines with them. In spite of the darkness, Ginny recognized Ben's muscular silhouette towering over her fallen attacker.

"Security! We need a hand over here!" Ben shouted.

As his voice boomed through the cavernous hangar, Ginny felt a stab of jealousy. Sure, when she'd tried to cry for help, no one could hear her over the sound of the plane engines. But now that the planes had left the building, Ben's words rang out clearly.

Hardly had Ben spoken when Earl Conklin, the Dare Divas' head security man, came running toward them from across the cavernous hangar, flashing on a bright Maglite as he ran. Zeke Ward, the top mechanic for the Dare Divas, dropped what he was working on and trotted over from his workbench along the far wall.

With the attacker out cold on the floor, Ben stepped closer. "Are you okay?"

Ginny felt the tender spot on her arm and winced. "I'm a lot better now. I'm surprised you made it in so fast."

"I figured I ought not to let you out of my sight for long." His hazel eyes locked on hers in the dim light, and Ginny saw wariness there. Either he didn't trust her to stick around long enough to finish their conversation, or he knew something of the trouble that had been following her. But how would he know that?

Earl's boots made a screeching sound against the polished cement floor as he skidded to a stop. "What happened here?"

"This guy—" Ben prodded the prone figure in the shoulder with his boot "—attacked Ginger."

Earl shined his light first at the unconscious attacker, then at Ben. "And who are you?"

"Ben McAlister," he introduced himself.

"Are you a relative of Ginger's?" Earl asked, obviously making the connection between Ben's last name and Ginny's flying moniker.

"Sort of," Ben answered, looking up at Ginny as though for confirmation.

They weren't related—not really. The closest family tie came through his cousin, who had married her brother. And the McAlisters weren't supposed to know she'd taken their name to fly under. Ginny was going to have to have a talk with her brother when she returned to Holyoake in two weeks. He was supposed to keep the details of her identity under wraps. She wouldn't have shared her secret with him if she'd thought he'd tell anyone.

She felt the fear, which had started to ease its grip when her attacker went down, tighten around her heart once again. She needed to get away from Ben—to get away from the whole situation. "He's okay," Ginny assured Earl, knowing the overzealous security man would likely have Ben thrown out if he thought Ben didn't belong there. Earl had been cracking down on security access ever since the trouble had started in New Jersey. But his efforts hadn't helped. Danger had followed them all the way to Wyoming—and continued to plague them, if the creepy guy out cold on the cement floor was any indication.

"Still—" Earl flashed his light back into Ben's face "—I'll need to ask you some questions."

"Sure." Ben shrugged agreeably, though his eyes were focused on Ginny and not on Earl.

Ginny felt her heart pounding out a staccato beat under his gaze. Much as she appreciated the way he'd rescued her from the attacker, she needed to get away from him to catch her breath.

"I—I think I need to sit down." She didn't have to fake the lightheaded feeling brought on by all that had just happened. "Please excuse me."

Earl had already begun to handcuff the unconscious attacker. As Ginny began to step around the man's motionless form, she felt Ben's strong arm brush her back. "Do you need a hand?" he offered, his deep voice causing her heart to beat erratically for an entirely different reason this time.

If she was honest, she could probably use a strong arm

to lean on for the walk back to her trailer. But she didn't want Ben McAlister getting any closer to her than he already had.

"I can help you to your trailer." Zeke Ward, the mechanic who'd been standing quietly by ever since Ben had called for help, stepped forward and took Ginny's arm.

"Thanks." Ginny smiled at the slightly built man, who stood a couple of inches shorter than she did. "I appreciate it."

Her words were almost buried by Earl's insistence. "I need to ask you some questions, *Ben McAlister.*" The way Earl said Ben's name, it sounded as though he didn't trust him, or didn't even believe he was who he said he was.

Ginny paused. Should she defend Ben? One look at the burly Air Force man told her he could defend himself. "Thank you," she told Ben quietly, meeting his eyes momentarily—just long enough to wonder at the intensity of his gaze.

Why had her brother sent Ben to fetch her? Was it really that important for her to return to Holyoake so soon? And most perplexing of all, why had Cutch told Ben about Ginny's pseudonym—her secret name that he'd promised never to reveal to anyone?

Too much didn't make sense.

But Ginny wasn't going to get any of it sorted out until she got away from Ben's distracting presence and collected her thoughts. She let Zeke accompany her to her trailer, glad to have someone nearby as she strode across the empty yard. Hadn't she always heard that it was safer to travel in pairs or groups than all alone? Zeke wasn't a terribly imposing figure, but at least he was someone.

And, it occurred to Ginny, he hadn't been far away when she was attacked. Perhaps he had seen something?

"Did you happen to notice how that man who attacked

me entered the hangar?" Ginny asked Zeke as they reached her trailer.

"Front door's wide open."

"You didn't notice him coming in, or standing there smoking?"

"I've had my hands full. No time to notice things."

Ginny looked over the mechanic, from his oil-stained jumpsuit to the stray wisps of sandy-colored hair that had long since given up trying to cover his head. The man's face was blank and guileless, but Ginny knew from all the years he'd traveled with the Dare Divas that underneath his unimpressive exterior, Zeke was a gifted mechanic. Could he be hiding other secrets?

Suddenly aware that she'd let herself be alone with the man, Ginny quickly thanked him for walking her to her trailer, and excused herself inside. Her heart was thumping hard by the time she closed the door behind her, relieved to see her friend, roommate and fellow stuntwoman Megan Doyle reading picture books to her four-year-old son on the sofa. The endearing image calmed Ginny's fright somewhat. She loved Megan and Noah and enjoyed sharing the trailer home with them.

"Are you okay?" Megan asked, looking up from her reading.

"I just need a shower," Ginny assured her with a smile.

"Okay." Megan sounded uncertain.

Ginny rushed to her room and grabbed things for the shower. She needed first of all to wash off the lingering smell of the sweaty smoker guy. And she needed a place to collect her thoughts before facing Ben McAlister again. She had a feeling he wouldn't easily back down on his plan to take her back to Iowa.

There was something about that man that made her heart do crazy things—even crazier than the fear-clenched pain she'd learned to live with lately. Though she felt she could trust him, Ben frightened her in ways all the death-defying stunts and stalkers in the world never could. For the first time since she'd left home at eighteen, she almost wanted to go back to Iowa. If Ben had the power to make her want to go home, she knew she had no choice but to get rid of him—fast.

TWO

Ben waited on the sofa for Ginny. He was glad he'd caught Ginny's roommate before she left, and even more relieved that Megan had so cheerfully agreed to let him wait inside the trailer. Of course, it didn't hurt that he was a McAlister. Apparently none of the Dare Divas realized that wasn't Ginny's real last name.

As was his habit ever since his Air Force training, he'd already scoped out the trailer home. It was pretty straightforward: one end was an open living area, which was separated by a countertop from a kitchenette. A hallway ran the length of the rest of the building past four doors, which he figured to be a bathroom and bedrooms, maybe a closet. Trailer homes weren't known for sophisticated architecture, though to its credit, the upscale model Ginny shared with Megan boasted a vaulted ceiling in the living room.

The walls, however, were completely bare, without a single picture to indicate anyone had had a chance to make the place feel like home. From what Ben understood of the situation, the Dare Divas flying troupe had relocated to Wyoming two months earlier, after trouble had chased them from New Jersey.

Ben had first seen them perform six years before when he'd been stationed at McGuire Air Force Base. Of course he'd noticed that the stunning redhead who led the troupe shared his last name. He'd just thought it was a funny co-incidence.

Maybe it was homesickness, maybe a sense of connection with the dazzling McAlister pilot, but Ben had managed to catch several other Dare Divas air shows over the years. He'd even been tempted to buy one of the posters of Ginger McAlister that seemed to sell out so quickly after every show. He'd never given in to the impulse, but he'd certainly taken his time admiring her smiling face on the poster before passing by. All along, he'd never suspected the gorgeous redhead was little Ginny McCutcheon from Holyoake, Iowa.

No one from Holyoake had suspected it, either, except for her brother Cutch, who'd made Ben promise not to tell anyone that Ginny flew for "some air show gig." It wasn't until Cutch had shown Ben a recent photograph of Ginny that Ben had realized the two redheaded pilots were really the same woman. When Cutch had told Ben about the accident involving Ginny's fellow pilot Kristy Keller, Ben had become concerned.

Prompted by Ben's concern, Cutch had done a quick search online. They'd both been alarmed by the events they read about in the incident listings in the Gillette, Wyoming, newspaper's online archive. Ginny had been shot at—twice. Other planes had been tampered with, though fortunately the damage had been caught before anyone else was injured. It was enough to convince them both that Ginny needed to come home to Holyoake before she was hurt by any of the attempts against the Dare Divas.

Cutch had decided Ginny should come home well ahead of the wedding celebration, and he'd quickly commissioned Ben to fetch his sister. Since Ben had recently stepped down after his last tour of service in the Air Force, he was more than happy to donate his time. He certainly didn't question that Ginny needed help. And from what he'd seen since his arrival, he was glad he'd gotten there when he did. Any later and Ginny might not have been there for him to find.

The doorknob rattled down the hall, pulling him from his worried thoughts. A cloud of steam billowed into the hallway as a door opened, followed by Ginny who, other than bare feet and the towel around her head, was fully dressed and didn't look quite as pale as she had when he'd last spoken to her. He could only pray this conversation would go better than the last one.

Ginny looked up as she entered the living room and jumped when she saw him. "Ben!" Her hand flew to her heart. "What are you doing in my trailer? How did you get in here?"

"Megan let me in."

"What was she thinking?" Ginny stomped over to the front door and tried the lock. "For all she knows you could be a creepy stalker guy." The door opened easily in her hands. Apparently Megan hadn't locked it on her way out. "Augh!" Ginny looked more than a little frustrated—she looked shaken. But then Ben figured she had every right to feel that way.

"I showed her my ID and explained that we're relatives."

"We're hardly relatives." Ginny scrunched up her nose at him as soon as she'd twisted the lock into place.

"My cousin married your brother," Ben reminded her as he stood and crossed the room, tired of trying to carry on the conversation with her halfway across the trailer home.

"Cutch married your cousin Elise in a private ceremony last fall so that my father could see them married before his cancer made him too sick to stand up. Now they're planning a big wedding celebration and I'm supposed to be a bridesmaid." She recited the facts as though she was still coming to grips with all that had happened. "So what does that make you? My cousin-in-law? That hardly qualifies as being related."

Ben grinned. He could tell Ginny was irritated with him, but he preferred seeing angry fire in her blue eyes rather than the hollow fear he'd sensed earlier, both in the hangar and on the prairie. He figured he might as well stoke that angry fire and watch the sparks fly. "Besides that, we share a last name," he reminded her.

That got the sparks shooting, all right. Ginny dropped her voice. "Nobody from Holyoake is supposed to know my flying name—nobody besides my brother, anyway." Anger and warning carried through in her tone. Ben had heard that Cutch's red-haired little sister was a feisty one. At least she didn't look like she was going to pass out anymore.

"Well, *I* know it." He smiled brightly. "And I have to say I'm more than a little curious about why you'd choose to take the McAlister name to fly under. You're a McCutcheon, not a McAlister."

Ginny pulled the sagging towel from her head and shook out her damp red mane. "Stunt flying isn't exactly a noble profession," she reported snappily. "It's like running off to join the circus. So I figured instead of embarrassing *my* family, I'd just embarrass yours."

Ben tried to follow her logic. He knew their families hadn't gotten along in generations, and he guessed there was more to that story than what she'd shared, but he hadn't traveled seven hundred miles just to hear her story. "I've seen you fly, Ginny. You've got nothing to be embarrassed about."

His compliment seemed to douse her defense. For the first time, she appeared to be at a loss for words.

"I'm sorry if I surprised you," he continued. "Your brother suggested things would go better if I didn't call ahead."

"If you'd called ahead, I wouldn't have been here when you arrived," Ginny assured him flatly, confirming her brother's prediction.

Ben sobered as he considered just how close she'd come to not being there. "Your brother's worried about you."

His simple statement appeared to shake her, though Ben couldn't fathom why the news would come as a surprise. "Cutch and Elise are both worried about you," he continued, watching her carefully as she absorbed the news. "You didn't come home for their wedding last fall. They don't want you to miss the wedding celebration, too."

"The ceremony last fall wasn't a real wedding." She looked up at him with sorrow in her eyes. "They just wanted to make it official before my dad died."

"They really are married, Ginny," Ben reminded her. "And they're going to be really disappointed if you don't make it back for the big celebration."

Ginny looked down at the floor and Ben thought he detected a slight tremble in her lower lip. He'd seen the pain that had crossed her face when she'd mentioned her father's death. He imagined that had probably been difficult for her, too. He could only pray that by knocking out the man who'd tried to carry her off, he might have finally eliminated one of the problems that plagued her. But he didn't want to wait around in Wyoming to find out.

"Come back to Holyoake with me, Ginny." He tried to meet her eyes and felt frustrated when she wouldn't look up at him. "You're supposed to be in a wedding."

"It's not for over two weeks." Ginny stepped farther away from him. "And it's not a real wedding."

Ben let her have her space, but he didn't back off. "You missed the real wedding. Are you planning to miss the celebration, too?"

The stubborn spark returned as she shot a look at him. "Of course I'll be there. I said I'd be there—in two weeks. But I've got work to do here. Just like I had work to do last fall when they called on short notice to announce they were getting hitched. I couldn't drop everything then, any more than I can take two weeks off now."

The last of her words broke off as loud pounding on the other side of the door startled Ginny.

"Ginny?" a concerned voice called from the other side. "It's Earl Conklin. I have two Campbell County sheriff's deputies with me. They'd like to ask you a few questions."

Suddenly Ginny stepped closer and placed her hand on Ben's arm. He felt her fingertips tremble as she held on to him like some kind of lifeline.

"Stay here while they question me." Vulnerability shimmered in her blue eyes. "Please?"

If she hadn't looked so frightened, he might have smiled at her request and the sudden contact of her hand on his arm. Instead he stated seriously, "I'm not leaving your side until we're back in Iowa."

A flicker of protest chased across her freckled features, but she didn't argue with him. Instead she offered up a forced smile and opened the door.

Ginny was glad to have Ben sitting beside her on the sofa as she faced Earl Conklin and the two local sheriff's deputies who'd accompanied him inside her trailer. She didn't think she had the strength to endure any more questions, but as long as she kept her hand on Ben's strong arm, she didn't feel so alone. Of course, she knew she had to get rid of Ben as soon as the officers left, but in the meantime, having Ben back up her story made all the difference to her peace of mind.

"You're sure you'd never seen him before?" Jim, one of the deputies, asked again about the man who'd attacked her in the hangar earlier.

Much as she wanted to make some sassy retort, she knew it wouldn't earn her any points with the investigator. And she knew the Campbell County sheriff's department had to resent the added burden on law enforcement that the Dare Divas had brought west with them. The deputies had already investigated the gunshots that had so narrowly missed her over the last few weeks, as well as dealing with disruptions from the battling news teams that were each trying to out-scoop the others' story. Jim and Roger, the other deputy, had probably spent more time at the Dare Diva training grounds than they had anywhere else lately.

Ginny bit her tongue and shook her head solemnly.

"I can't recall ever seeing the man," she insisted. "But as you know, the Dare Divas perform before thousands of spectators. I never see most of my fans, except from high in the air. He may have been at every show and I wouldn't know it."

The officers nodded and continued making notes. Earl scowled and Ginny could almost see his mind working as he tried to think of a question he could ask that would make all the pieces fall into place, that would make all their troubles go away.

Poor Earl. He'd been under so much pressure, especially since Kristy's accident. No one blamed him that the attack took place on his watch. And Ginny didn't blame him now. But she could tell from the distraught expression on his face that he continued to blame himself.

"That's all the questions we have." Roger, the taller officer, nodded to Earl.

The men started to stand, and Ginny felt relieved that they were finally going to leave.

Then Ben cleared his throat. "What can you tell us about the suspect in this afternoon's attack?"

The deputies sat back down and Ginny stifled her sigh. Though she hoped the investigators would get to the bottom of the Dare Divas' troubles, just thinking of her attacker made her feel sick. She didn't care to know anything about the man. She'd prefer to forget the incident had ever occurred. Mostly she wanted everyone to leave, including Ben. But that wasn't going to happen as long as people kept asking questions.

The taller deputy looked solemn. "He'll be interviewed as soon as he's had the opportunity to contact his lawyer. But according to his ID, his name is Bobby Burbank, from Folsom, New Jersey."

"Folsom!" Ginny repeated in spite of herself. The town was just up the road from Atlantic City, the Dare Divas' east coast address. The flying troupe traditionally operated out of New Jersey and had been headquartered there year-round until the difficulties there had sent them flying for the relative safety and isolation of their training grounds in Wyoming. But trouble had obviously followed them. "Our move to Wyoming wasn't made public."

Jim's smile seemed to mock her. "It's kind of hard to hide a troupe of three dozen stunt-flying women."

Ginny closed her eyes and kept her mouth shut, reminding herself that the men weren't going to go away as long as she kept talking.

"Anything else you can tell us about him?" Ben asked.

"Nothing that you haven't observed for yourself already." The taller officer stood. "We'll let you know if we uncover anything pertinent to the case." Earl and Jim stood with him.

Ginny hurried to see them to the door, forcing herself to thank them in spite of the frustration she felt. Getting upset wouldn't help anything. She pulled the door open and saw Veronica and Jasmine, two of her fellow Dare Divas, headed toward her trailer from across the barren yard.

"Ginger!" Veronica called. "Are the sheriff's deputies with you?"

"They're right here," Ginny called across the yard to her friends as the men stepped outside.

Jasmine broke into a run at the sight of the deputies, and Veronica picked up her pace as well. When Ginny glanced at Jim and Roger, she saw them smiling. Well, who wouldn't be, with two lovely young women beaming up at them the way Veronica and Jasmine were?

"We found a car!" Jasmine announced in a breathless voice.

"It's a rental car." Veronica came to a stop next to her. "We don't recognize it. Do you think the man who attacked Ginny might have driven it here?"

The deputies exchanged glances with one another.

"We can take a look at it," Jim offered. "Lead the way."

Earl followed the two sheriff's deputies as they hurried across the yard after the girls. Ben, as promised, stayed by Ginny's side as she closed the door after them, wishing she could just as easily shut all the trouble out of her life.

She could feel Ben's questioning eyes resting on her, but she didn't have the strength to look up. It had been such a trying day—such a trying three months since Kristy's accident. She managed to lift her eyes high enough to take in Ben's broad shoulders and muscular chest. For a moment, she wondered what it would be like to rest her head on those strong shoulders and have a good, long cry.

Now where had that thought come from? She hardly knew Ben McAlister. Besides, she needed to figure out how to get rid of him. If she let him see how frightened she was, he'd never let her stay in Wyoming.

"Thank you for all of your help today," she said evenly. "I'm sorry I won't be able to go back to Iowa with you." She risked a glance into Ben's eyes and wished she hadn't. His green-and-brown eyes looked angry, maybe even hurt. She took a gulp and pressed on. "I'm sure my brother will understand."

"He doesn't understand, and neither does Elise. She thinks you don't like her."

Ginny felt her mouth make a round O, but she couldn't make any sound come out. She hadn't meant to snub her new sister-in-law. In fact, she was hoping to get along well with her once she got to Iowa. Surely her brother and his new wife didn't take too much offense at her waiting a little while longer to return home.

She met Ben's eyes and tried not to think about how the muddied green in his hazel eyes reminded her of flying over the fields of Iowa in June. The fields back home would look like that now, wouldn't they? She shook off the thought.

"I can come a few days early. Instead of that Friday morning, how about the Wednesday before the wedding? That should allow plenty of time for a dress fitting and a party or two."

"It would be better if you came now," Ben said flatly. He looked less than pleased. The muscles in his shoulders flexed, and it occurred to Ginny that the big ex-military man could easily throw her over his shoulder and carry her off to Iowa if he wanted to. He was plenty stronger than the man who'd attacked her that afternoon.

"Ben, please." She rested one hand on his forearm, the same arm she'd clung to throughout the interview with the local authorities. Unlike her attacker from earlier, she knew Ben would be civilized. She sensed that she could trust him.

But how much could she trust him? There were days when she felt she couldn't trust anyone anymore. What if this Bobby Burbank fellow wasn't behind all the attacks on the troupe? What if the trouble that had followed the Dare Divas to Wyoming continued to follow her home? She couldn't bring danger back to Holyoake. How could she ever forgive herself if something happened to someone? At least here in Wyoming, everyone was aware of the danger, and their security team was hard at work to find the culprit. She looked into those hazel June-field eyes.

"There is more at stake here than just a wedding." If her voice sounded pleading, so be it. She had to make him understand. She wouldn't put the people of Holyoake in danger by spending more time back home than was necessary. And she needed to stay in Wyoming to keep in the loop with their security team—for everyone's safety. "Don't make this more difficult than it already is. I can't go to Iowa any sooner than that."

Ben looked down into Ginny's blue eyes and wondered. Did she understand the danger she was in? Until he knew for certain that Bobby Burbank had been solely responsible for every attack on the Dare Divas, Ben wasn't about to dismiss the threats against her life. Should he just come out and tell her the real reason he wanted her to leave

Wyoming now—because he feared her life was being threatened? Or would explaining his fears only frighten her more? She looked like she'd already been through all she could handle.

Frustrated, Ben wished he knew more about how to read women, or at least how to talk to them. But growing up without any sisters, he'd never learned that skill. During his years in the Air Force, he'd naturally gravitated toward his fellow males who outnumbered the women four to one in that line of service. He was way out of his comfort zone and unsure how to proceed. The only plan he could see was to fall back and regroup, and pray nothing bad happened to Ginny before he brought her home.

"I'm sorry," he apologized. "I know you've had a rough day."

Relief filled her features.

"I'll head into Gillette and try to find a hotel—"

"Don't bother." When Ginny interrupted him, he thought at first she was going to tell him to get lost. But she continued, "It's tourist season. Unless you have a reservation, you won't find a room on a Friday evening. We've got a couple of empty trailers here. Let me find Ron or Doug Adolph. They're the owners and managers of the Dare Divas. One of them will find you a place to stay."

Ben smiled at her offer. So she wasn't chasing him off?

"Did you fly that plane up from Holyoake? You'll need a good night's rest to make it back to Iowa tomorrow."

"I flew straight out," Ben admitted, stuffing his hands in his pockets, forcing himself to keep mum about the rest of Ginny's inference. He wasn't going back to Iowa tomorrow—not unless she was with him. But there was obviously no point arguing about it any more. He'd let her find him a trailer to stay in, and then he'd hunker down until she agreed to return to Holyoake.

In spite of her exhaustion, Ginny had difficulty falling asleep that night. Pain, her constant companion ever since Kristy's accident, seared through her chest. Her doctors had done every sort of test, but the only source they could find for her troubles was stress.

That much made sense. The endless fear she felt was stressful enough. The attempts on her life only reinforced the fear and the pain that came with it. And now Ben's arrival from Holyoake gave her plenty more to worry about. Though the trailer he was staying in was nearly fifty feet away from hers, Ginny felt the weight of Ben's presence and all that he'd told her.

She'd hoped Cutch and Elise would be so caught up in wedding plans that they wouldn't mind if she didn't arrive until right before the wedding. Obviously she'd underestimated their level of distraction. They'd only had eyes for each other when Ginny had been home to visit her dad a couple of times as his cancer spread, leading to his death. And the newlywed pair had only briefly spoken to her when she'd been home for her father's funeral. But then again, she'd only been in Iowa for a little over four hours—just enough time to give everyone a hug, sip some coffee at the luncheon afterward and get back to New Jersey in time for their last show.

As it was, she'd arrived at the air show later than she'd intended. Kristy Keller had filled in, flying Ginny's plane for the opening segment of the show.

Which was why Kristy had been at the controls when the engine had cut out and the plane had gone down—and why Kristy, instead of Ginny, now lay in a burn unit.

Ginny buried her head under her pillow, letting the silent

tears soak into the sheets as they slipped from her cheeks. There had been a time when such sobs would have been accompanied by fervent prayers to God. After all, wasn't that how she'd responded every time her mother had called with a new report on her father's nine-year battle with cancer? Praying in faith that God would heal her father, praying to a God who she thought actually cared.

Her faith had been buried with her father. Kristy's accident had sealed the tomb. And her fears over the attacks on the Dare Divas? She hadn't figured out how to handle those, which was why the pain in her heart wouldn't go away.

An acrid tang seared through her slumber as she slept fitfully, her dreams filled with anger and darkness. She could still smell the smoke of Bobby Burbank's cigarette, could still feel his choking arms around her.

And she could hear cries and the sound of breaking glass.

"Ginny!" It was Ben's voice, and Ben's strong arms lifting her.

Ginny tried to open her eyes, but the smoke burned them. "What?" Her mind raced back over the twisted paths of her dream. She wasn't in the hangar, she was in her trailer. But it was on fire, smoke alarms blaring, and Ben held her tight to his chest as he stepped carefully through her broken bedroom window.

"It's okay. Megan and Noah already escaped. You're going to be fine." Ben's deep voice rumbled soothingly near her ear.

Ginny gulped fresh air as Ben stepped outside with her cradled in his arms. What had happened? Why was the trailer on fire? She tried to push away from Ben, but he held her securely.

"You're okay. I've got you." His strong arms stilled her struggles.

As she became more alert, she realized Ben had arrived just in time. Flames crackled around them and smoke filled the air.

"Ginger!" Megan ran toward them, four-year-old Noah clasping her like a rhesus monkey clinging to its mother. "I'm so glad Ben found you! When I heard the smoke alarm, all I could think of was getting Noah to safety. When Ben came outside, I told him I thought you were still in there. I can't believe he made it through that fire. The flames were so thick!"

Ginny looked up at Ben and blinked away the tears that had formed in response to the fire's searing smoke. "Don't you know you're never supposed to go into a burning building?" She tried to tease him, but smoke tickled her throat, and she coughed.

"I didn't have much choice." The intensity in his expression surprised her. Though he'd set her down and no longer held her, he still stood awkwardly close.

She wanted to protest, to tell him a smart person would have left well enough alone, but the smoke continued to irritate her throat, and she found herself coughing as security personnel, firemen and her fellow stunt pilots swarmed the area around the trailer.

"Stay back!" Earl Conklin shouted, flashing his Maglite at the crowd. "This fire will need to be investigated. Don't anyone contaminate the area."

For a second, Earl faced the firefighters, and Ginny wondered if he wasn't going to try to keep them at bay with his flashlight, too. But he stepped out of their way just before they unleashed the full power of their hoses on the fire.

Ben's arms wrapped around her from behind, pulling

her back several steps, away from the fire and the firefighters' spray. Ginny stiffened instinctively, but quickly realized the sensibility of his actions. He had to be freezing in the chilly Wyoming night in only his lightweight flannel pajamas. She was cold, too, though her thick fleece sweats and insulated socks were more suited to the cold temperatures that were common at night in their high altitude, even in June. Forcing herself to relax, she leaned back against him and could feel the steady thump of his heartbeat against her back. So different from the pain-clenched pounding of her heart.

Still not comfortable looking him in the face, she stood in silence and watched the firemen battle the blaze, her attention torn between watching the ghastly scene in front of her and wondering about the heroic man who stood so close behind her. Ben had served in the Air Force for years, hadn't he? He was probably used to saving people's lives on a daily basis.

But Ginny wasn't used to being rescued. And she especially wasn't used to getting so close to a man, especially a man she'd admired for so long. She wasn't sure how to react.

Fortunately the firefighters provided plenty of distraction, and soon paramedics with thick blankets found them. Once Ben had his own blanket, Ginny stepped away from him, finally daring to turn and face him in the strobing red and blue light from the emergency vehicles. Though she was glad to put some physical distance between herself and the handsome military man, she still wasn't prepared for the way her stomach swooped when she met his eyes, which held an intense kindness in their green-and-brown depths.

The man had saved her life. She knew she needed to thank him, but it took her several moments to find her voice. Mustering words, she stumbled over a simple "thank you" and offered him a meager smile before retreating toward where Megan and Noah stood, feeling as though she'd utterly failed to express her gratitude.

But what else could she do? There was a part of her that wanted to hug the man. But a much bigger part of her felt terrified at the very idea of getting that close to him.

Ben talked to Earl, the deputies, the firefighters and anyone else who cared to share their theories with him. He didn't like any of the things he learned. Much as Ben had hoped that he'd ended Ginny's troubles when he'd knocked Bobby Burbank out cold, the fact that her trailer had nearly burned down while the man was behind bars told Ben that Ginny's life was still in danger. And according to the deputies, Bobby Burbank had been clocked in at work back in New Jersey when the previous shots had been fired at Ginny in Wyoming. So even if Bobby was behind those attacks, he couldn't have been working alone.

The only good news was that, with her trailer burned to the ground, Ginny might be slightly more inclined to return to Iowa with him. It was a small consolation. He found Ginny huddled under her blanket on the stoop of the trailer he'd been staying in, and he slumped down beside her.

"Looks like arson," he said quietly.

Ginny pinched her eyes shut tight. "I was afraid of that."

But that wasn't all he wanted to discuss. "Do you have any idea who's trying to kill you?" he asked.

Her eyes popped open and he saw fear there.

"I wasn't sure that anyone was." Her voice faltered.

Kicking himself for being so blunt, Ben once again wished he'd learned how to talk to a woman before it had become so critical. He tried to make his voice sound gentler, less accusing. "You've been shot at twice in the last three weeks."

"It was probably just some hunters who didn't realize how far their bullets traveled through the woods." The words sounded a little too practiced.

"And they just happened to shoot when you were the only one around—both times?"

Ginny didn't meet his eyes. "How do you know about the shootings?"

"Public record," Ben said bluntly. "Your brother was worried about you. The Gillette *News-Record* has online archives. Earl and the deputies filled in the rest." When she didn't comment, Ben cleared his throat. "The fire appears to have originated under the trailer. Care to guess which room it started under?"

Fear filled Ginny's face. Her voice sounded weak. "Mine?"

She sounded so lost, so alone, Ben couldn't stand it. He wrapped his arms around her, blanket and all, and pulled her against his shoulder.

He could feel the frantic beating of her heart, its erratic pulse even wilder than when he'd first rescued her. They watched in silence as the firefighters packed up their equipment to leave. Faint streaks of green lightened the eastern horizon. The sun would be rising soon. The shell of the trailer smoked, but the fire, at least, was out.

"What's going on, Ginny?" he whispered after he felt her pulse rate finally begin to even out.

She shook her head against his chest but said nothing.

"I want to help you," he said finally, "but you're keeping a lot of secrets from me."

Finally she looked up at him. Tears poured down her cheeks.

"Come back to Holyoake with me."

Fear shot through her eyes. "And bring trouble home? No way."

At her words, Ben felt all the anger that had built up inside him when he'd argued with Ginny the day before begin to drain away. Did she think she had to stay away from her family in order to protect them from whoever was after the Divas? Now her stubborn refusal to return home made perfect sense. But he still didn't like it.

"Ginny, you can't face these threats alone."

"Why not? I've made it this far, haven't I?"

Ben leaned back and regarded her tear-streaked face, from her disheveled red hair to a soot smudge on her freckled chin. So this was the real Ginger McAlister, the fearless aviatrix he'd revered for so long. He felt a tug on his heart that was unlike anything he'd ever known in all his thirty-eight years of bachelorhood.

And then he pulled her tight against his shoulder again. "I'm going to keep you safe, Ginny McCutcheon. Come back to Holyoake with me. Please?"

They sat in silence for several more long minutes. Ben considered it a victory that Ginny didn't automatically turn him down. A gust of wind carried through the airfield and they both startled as they watched the wall to Ginny's bedroom collapse inward.

Her shoulders rose and fell against him as she sucked in a couple of big breaths. Finally she said quietly, "Okay."

THREE

The sun was just beginning to rise as Ben helped Ginny pull back the tarp that covered the snub-nosed biplane hidden in a Quonset hut on the far edge of the Dare Divas' Wyoming property. When she'd requested to fly her own plane back to Iowa, Ben had readily agreed. By leaving his plane in Wyoming, he had an excuse to come back with her after the wedding—to get his plane, and to do whatever he could to keep her safe for as long as she'd let him.

As they pulled off the tarp, Ben saw that the sunny yellow plane gleamed from its last polish, but what caught his attention were the metal handles that protruded along the wings. His hand slid along the wing to the nearest handle, which looked like a bent stretch of rebar that had been welded to the plane, then painted yellow to match the rest of the craft.

He met Ginny's eyes.

"She's an old wing-walker," Ginny explained. "Custom-built for me and my acrobats."

Ben had seen enough Dare Divas air shows to understand what she meant. "These handles are so your passengers can climb out mid-flight and have something to hang on to while they're doing a gymnastics routine on the wings?" He shook his head. He'd spent his career flying combat missions, but that was inside a plane.

Ginny smiled at him. "It's a death-defying stunt," she acknowledged. "That's what makes it so thrilling to watch."

"You wouldn't catch me climbing outside the cockpit mid-flight. Not for money, not for anything."

"I thought you were a brave Air Force pilot." Her voice carried a teasing tone.

"I spent a twenty-year career in the sky." He met her eyes. "That's why I know enough to stay inside the cockpit."

He helped her inspect the plane prior to their flight. After all the "accidents" that had taken place around the troupe recently, Ben insisted on checking every plug and wire of the engine. He wasn't going to relax until Ginny was safely back in Iowa.

It seemed Ginny was focused on safety, too. She took her time going over the pre-flight check. Ben watched her from between the bi-wings, her expression intent, her blue eyes focused.

She was a joy to watch—not only when she performed in the air, but whatever she was doing. And she was uncompromisingly thorough with the pre-flight check. Ben appreciated that.

The pre-flight check completed, Ben was finally convinced the solid little plane would keep them in the sky just fine. Ginny had done a great job of maintaining it.

"How soon do you want to leave?"

Ginny shrugged. "Let me say goodbye to Megan and Noah. I'd pack a bag, but..." She trailed off as she looked back in the direction of the burnt-out trailer.

He understood, and offered her what he hoped was an encouraging smile. Really, it was remarkable the way she'd bounced back, though from the defeated slump of her shoulders he knew she felt more like she'd given up by agreeing to return to Holyoake with him. But right now he cared more about keeping her alive and keeping his promise to Cutch and Elise than he cared about her feelings of obligation to the Divas. After all she'd been through, he doubted there was much he could do to make her feel better anyway.

"I'm going to stay right here and keep an eye on the plane," Ben told her. "You go and do what you need to. I'll be right here."

She cast him an appreciative smile as she hurried off in the direction of the trailer Megan and Noah had moved into. Fortunately, the Doyles had been able to salvage most of their things, since the fire had been concentrated in the area of Ginny's room.

Ginny disappeared from sight, her slender form already familiar enough to Ben. Well, he'd gotten a head start from studying her picture on her posters all those years. In all that time, he'd never so much as considered the possibility that he'd ever meet Ginger McAlister.

He'd imagined her brave, fearless, maybe even a bit of a self-centered diva, as the flying troupe's name implied. But none of the stunt fliers he'd met so far were anything but sweet and good-natured. And Ginny didn't seem to be a diva—a fact Ben was glad for. Women were enough of a mystery to him. High-maintenance women left him completely at a loss.

Pulling out his cell phone, Ben gave Cutch a call, leaving a message to let him know they'd soon be on their way. Then he turned the phone over to check the time, and was disappointed to see that Ginny had been gone for nearly half an hour. They'd planned to leave early enough to be back in Holyoake in time for lunch. That part had been Ginny's idea.

So where was she? Recalling the trouble Ginny had encountered in the hangar the day before, Ben kicked himself for letting Ginny run off alone.

She could be in trouble! Abandoning his post guarding the plane, Ben struck off in the direction Ginny had disappeared, his heart hammering out a prayer for her safety.

There was no sign of anyone in the trailer Megan and Noah had moved into. Ginny wasn't at the main hangar or anywhere near the burnt remains of her trailer. Where could she be? Was she in trouble? Why had he let her go off by herself? He resolved to stick closer to her until they reached the safety of Holyoake—assuming he ever found her.

Ben checked the doors of buildings he hadn't been in before, and finally found a crowd of people milling in the large meeting room inside a Morton building that appeared to house offices for some of the Dare Divas staff. He finally spotted Ginny toward the front of the crowd.

Ron Adolph, the co-owner of the Dare Divas, whom Ben had met briefly the evening before, stood next to Ginny, making a speech of some sort. Ben had trouble making out the man's words in the crowded room, but his eyes narrowed as he took in the scene.

As Ben understood it, Ron had functioned as the ringmaster for the early Dare Divas shows, and had fostered their early popularity in part on his skill at working up excitement among the spectators. He still struck Ben as a bit of a snake oil salesman—someone who knew how to work a crowd into a fervor with his words. Was that what the man was doing now? Using Ginny as a prop to reassure the rest of his flying troupe? Or was Ben just being overly suspicious in his eagerness to sort out who was behind the attempts on Ginny's life?

Making his way past the gathered women to the front of the room, Ben finally reached Ginny's side. When she first looked up at him, he saw fear and uncertainty in her expression, but he watched as a smile filled her face the moment she recognized him. An unfamiliar feeling rose inside his heart as her eyes warmed. Did she trust him? Did she feel closer to him than to this man she'd worked for over the last eight years?

Ben didn't have time to puzzle it out.

He leaned down and whispered into her ear. "Daylight's wasting."

She nodded knowingly, and when Ron paused in his speech, Ginny waved to the assembled women. "Thank you. Thank you all for your support and friendship. I won't be gone long, but hopefully by the time I get back, these incidents..." Her voice caught and she looked up at Ben.

He placed a hand at her back, wanting to support her, to encourage her, somehow, though he wasn't sure what his role was, or what the flying girls must think of his sudden appearance in the midst of all the trouble they'd been having. Ginny had insisted on not telling *anyone* where she was headed, and Ben had earnestly agreed. Until they knew who was behind the attacks, he wanted to keep her under cover. Easier said than done.

"We'll sort it out," Ginny finished, her voice sounding a little lost.

The girls gave a cheer and someone started clapping, and soon the whole room was filled with young ladies showing their support for Ginny. Ben took a step back and watched aviatrix Ginger McAlister bid farewell to her fellow fliers. Funny, but he could almost see where little

Ginny ended and her flying persona began. She lifted a confident chin and gave the girls a poster-worthy grin.

When she looked back at him, he saw the glamour that had dazzled so many crowds over the years, and behind it, in the shadows of her eyes, the fear that had haunted her for months.

And suddenly he wished that he'd come sooner, that he'd gotten to know her better, that somehow he could have done something to keep her from having to experience all the trials she'd been through lately. His hands flexed anxiously, eager to shield her from view, as though by enfolding her in his arms he could guard her. If only it was that simple.

The best he could do was try to keep her safe from here on out. That meant getting her out of Wyoming and back to the safety of Holyoake before anything else could happen to her.

She gave him a nod and stepped past him. He placed a protective hand at her back, ushering her through the crowd, waiting patiently while she stopped to hug several of her fellow fliers on her way out. Ben studied the girls who hugged her and the girls who held back, recognizing Veronica, one of the two women who'd arrived at the trailer the day before. He didn't see Jasmine anywhere, though it appeared as though nearly everyone associated with the Dare Divas had crammed into the metal building.

Veronica and Jasmine had proven to be helpful the day before. As he'd later learned from the sheriff's deputies, the car the two women had spotted had indeed been rented to Bobby Burbank, but unfortunately its discovery didn't yield any more answers. All they had were questions.

Who was behind the attacks on the troupe, including the attempts on Ginny's life? Did one of the smiling faces in the room hide a jealous heart? Did one of Ginny's fellow fliers want her job as the face of the Dare Divas Barnstorming Troupe? Was it a role worth killing for?

Ben wouldn't rule out any possibilities. He felt certain Ginny wouldn't really be safe until the person behind the attacks on her life was locked away. And based on the fire the night before, Ben doubted Bobby Burbank could have been behind everything—at least, not working alone.

When they finally stepped out of the crowded building, Ben took a deep breath of the crisp Wyoming air and looked down in time to see Ginny doing the same.

"Sorry that took so long."

He shrugged off her concern. "We need to head out."

They hurried back to the Quonset where they'd left the yellow biplane. The undersized enclosed cabin had room for one pilot up front, and a bench seat in the back that would accommodate Ben with room to spare, though he suspected it had probably held more than a few wingwalking acrobats during its years of service.

Ben pitched his bag into the back seat and was surprised to see Ginny had acquired a backpack since she'd first left him.

"The girls put together some things for me." She sounded touched by their gesture.

"That was thoughtful." Ben paused, so many questions swirling in his mind, but really, there was no time to ask them.

Ginny tossed Ben a headset before sliding her flying helmet on and tucking in her thick red hair. He appreciated her thoughtfulness. The headset would allow him to converse with her easily over the ambient noise inside the cabin of the small plane. Ginny's radio communication device was part of her flying helmet. Ben recognized it as being top of the line.

Once she had her helmet on and her head up, Ginny

opened her mouth as though she might say something to him, but then gave her head a slight shake and stepped past him to the pilot's seat. Ben settled in on the bench seat behind her and wondered what she'd been about to say.

With his muscular six-foot-three-inch frame, Ben felt a little cramped in the small cabin of the plane, but it was nothing he wasn't used to after all the hours he'd logged flying in his career. Angling his body diagonally across the seat, he rested his head against the curved enclosure of the cabin and found he could comfortably watch Ginny at the controls.

He'd enjoyed every air show he'd ever watched her fly in, but this was something new entirely—the opportunity to see her at work, up close. The woman clearly knew what she was doing, and Ben found himself immediately at ease with the plane in her capable hands.

Their takeoff was smooth in spite of the hardened turf that served as their runway, but then, Ben figured Ginny was familiar enough with the terrain. Since the Dare Divas often flew shows at fairs and other impromptu venues, he knew they needed to be skilled at taking off from grass and fields. Their Wyoming training grounds offered plenty of opportunity to practice, without the crowded New Jersey airspace they were sure to encounter out east.

As he understood it, the Dare Divas lived close to population centers for much of the year so they could quickly travel to air shows, but during the gaps in their schedule, they stayed busy practicing and perfecting new routines on the sparsely populated high plains of eastern Wyoming.

Now the land fell away beneath them as Ginny pointed the plane toward Iowa, and home. The plane ride went quickly.

Ben watched the beautiful Badlands of South Dakota come into view as they left northeast Wyoming behind on their way to southwest Iowa. The scenery was spectacular, and Ben appreciated the opportunity to enjoy the landscape from a vantage point few got to see. Ginny kept the plane at a fairly low altitude, offering them both an unparalleled view of the rugged terrain.

After a while, Ben felt his stomach growl. "Hungry?" he asked, opening his bag and pulling out a box of granola bars.

"Sometimes I forget to eat," Ginny confessed.

"I rarely have that problem." Ben sorted through the variety pack. "Chocolate chip, cinnamon or peanut butter?"

"Mmm, chocolate chip."

He opened the bar for her and placed it in her out-stretched hand.

"Thanks." She took a quick bite. "I don't want to take my hands off the controls. I think we're entering a turbulent patch."

"I can feel it." The vibrations were subtle so far, and Ginny was doing a great job of keeping the plane smooth in spite of them, but Ben knew the air like a farmer knew his fields. And he was pretty certain things were going to get bumpier before they got better. "I don't like the look of those clouds."

"I've seen worse," Ginny assured him, tearing off another bite of granola.

Ben grinned and settled in. He was in good hands. A lot of people tended to get on his nerves while traveling, but so far, Ginny had proven to be remarkably easy to get along with. And it didn't hurt that she was nice to look at, too.

Suddenly the plane lurched and Ben bounced in his seat. He thought about making a teasing comment, but one glimpse of Ginny's white-knuckled grip on the controls told him now was not the time to distract her. He sat farther forward in his seat, hoping to read the instruments over her shoulder, but the bouncing plane made it nearly impossible for him to focus.

He looked at the looming storm clouds building like a wall in front of them.

"I'm going to take her lower," Ginny said, her voice as tense as her grip.

"Good idea," Ben agreed. He wasn't sure exactly where they were, though he suspected at some point they'd crossed into Nebraska. They were likely over the sand hills somewhere—the Great American Desert, the early settlers used to call it. Ben had loved studying maps growing up, a hobby that had served him well over the years. Now he tried to picture where they were flying—over some of the least inhabited land between Wyoming and Iowa, and that was saying something.

"I still don't like the look of those clouds." Ben watched the looming forms draw nearer.

"Neither do I." Ginny's voice was little more than a whisper, and Ben could hear the strain behind her words. "But what other choice do I have? There's no cover if we land now—and that storm is coming for us. Those cumulonimbus clouds could be hiding hail. Our best bet is to keep her in the air. I've flown through worse."

"So have I. You're doing great." His words barely made it from his lips as the plane hit the storm front, which seemed to pluck up their tiny plane and toss it in the air.

As Ben watched, Ginny bounced high in her seat, straining the limits of her harness, then came down with a groan.

Ben blinked. The instrument panel had gone dark, and all indicators pointed to zero.

"What happened to the engine?" Ben asked as the eerie whistling of the wind replaced the sound of the motor.

"I don't know." Ginny's fingers fumbled at the ignition. "We're dead in the air."

Ben reached past Ginny and tried to get the engine to turn over. He couldn't hear anything amidst the rising screams from the storm, but the instrument panel was completely unresponsive.

"Get back in your seat," Ginny barked at him. "Buckle up. I'm going to try to land her."

With little other option before him, Ben decided to trust the red-headed woman and her skills with the plane. He didn't like the idea of landing in this storm, especially without an engine, but if anyone had asked him the pilot he'd trust to execute such a move, he'd have told them aviatrix Ginger McAlister. Silently he started to pray.

Ginny couldn't see. It wasn't just the swirling sand and wind, which were bad enough, but the dark cloud cover and complete lack of instruments gave her *nothing* to go on. She felt her pulse pounding in her head, felt her heart clenching as though it might stop beating altogether. Like the engine of her plane.

What had happened? She didn't have time to sort it out. Her only hope was to get the plane on the ground in one piece, if that was possible. For now, she was glad about the sucking turbulence that picked up the plane and swept it aloft like a leaf caught in an updraft. Anything to keep them from smashing to the ground.

She kept their nose pointed slightly up. They'd come down on their belly. She'd lost position some time ago, but based on dead reckoning, she judged them to be somewhere over the western section of the Nebraska sand hills.

Nothing like trying to land a lifeless plane in rolling sand dunes.

A sudden gust grabbed her right wing, spinning her sideways.

"We're upside-down." Ben's voice sounded remarkably level.

She'd have shot back a smart retort, but every cell in her body was focused on getting the plane righted. It wasn't built to land upside down, though she'd at least had plenty of practice flying that way.

When the next gust hit, she let go of the controls completely and let the plane spin free. When her stomach settled back into its natural position, she grabbed the handles of the steering wheel and cranked hard back into the turn.

They leveled out.

Now if only she had some way of telling how close they were to the ground.

The rounded dome of a sand dune skimmed by beneath them.

Just in time, Ginny picked up the nose as they sank, skidding across the next dune with a jolt that pressed her body so hard against the five-point harness she was certain she'd have bruises in the outline of the nylon straps. The plane slid sideways down the hill, but there was nothing Ginny could do any more to influence which way they went or even whether they rolled.

The plane shimmied down the hill on its belly, skidding across the sand and sparse scrub grass, coming to rest with one wingtip slicing into the next hill. The inclined sides of the valley offered some protection from the wind that howled above them.

Before she'd even caught her breath, Ben's hands reached around her and unbuckled her harness.

"What—" she started to ask.

"Get out!" He cut her off abruptly.

She wanted to remind him that a sandstorm was raging outside, but she understood his impulse. They didn't know what had caused their engine to cut out. They didn't know what might have been damaged on impact, or even if someone had tampered with the plane. But Ginny was fairly certain they still had a pretty full tank of fuel—more than enough to blow a big hole in the sand dunes if a spark hit it. Just such an explosion had followed Kristy's crash. In her case, spectators, including a few off-duty firemen, had rushed to the scene and managed to pull her out alive.

There were no spectators in the Great American Desert. Ginny knew she and Ben would have to get out on their own—fast.

Given the sideways tilt of the plane, Ginny all but fell into Ben's arms as soon as she slid out of her harness. She reached behind him for her backpack as they spilled out the door. Ben scooped her up as she stumbled, and he pulled her around the side of the dune, just out of sight of the plane. They hunkered down close against the screaming wind.

Ginny panted hard as she leaned against Ben's shoulder and tried to catch her breath. Her lungs screamed with the same pain that clenched at her heart. That had been so close. Way too close. Fear clawed through her chest.

Her knees weak, she sagged downward and welcomed an excuse to touch the solid earth, to hug it if she could. But Ben pulled her upright and she slumped against him instead. At least his broad shoulders gave her something solid to hang onto.

"Your heart is beating like a scared rabbit's."

Ginny gulped a couple of deep breaths. "I am a scared

rabbit." She pressed her face into his shirt to protect her eyes from the swirling sand.

She pulled in a few more breaths and willed her heart to beat with the same strong, steady rhythm she felt thumping away in Ben's chest.

It did nothing.

Fortunately, the stalwart circle of Ben's arms around her didn't waver. After a while, his voice rumbled near her ear. "You think the plane's okay?"

She kept her face tight against him for protection from the flying sand, but let her mouth move closer to his ear. "Other than being crashed in the sand, I guess it's okay. I didn't hear an explosion."

"Good." Ben's arms loosened their grip on her. "I'm going to go check it out."

"What do you mean?"

"I mean, we need to figure out why the engine cut out so suddenly mid-flight. You and I both inspected that plane thoroughly." He turned his face until his forehead pressed against hers, effectively blocking the stinging sand that swirled around them.

Ginny risked blinking her eyes open. Whoa. Ben's muddy hazel eyes stared down at her, so close. She suddenly realized the position she was in, protected by his strong arms from the storm that raged around them. He was closer than she ever let anyone get. Her knees felt suddenly weak, but not from the crash this time.

"G-good idea." She let go of him and tucked her head into the bent crook of her arm, following him as he made his way through the deep sand to the plane.

The way the yellow bird had landed, the engine was sheltered by the bi-wings and the steep sides of the dune, forming a protected cove where the wind didn't whistle nearly so loudly, and the sand didn't swirl so much.

Ben's fingers found the severed cord just as Ginny spotted it.

"No," she protested, taking in the worn-through casing around the power output wire that looked as though it had snapped—probably when the plane had lurched in the turbulence. "Those casings were solid. I felt the whole length of that wire when we inspected the plane prior to take-off."

Ben shook his head regretfully. "I should never have left the plane unattended."

Ginny wouldn't let him blame himself. "You only left the plane to come look for me." And even that hadn't been for long. Whoever had tampered with the plane must have been watching, waiting for an opening. Ginny could have kicked herself for not checking the plane again when they returned to it. She'd almost suggested to Ben that they do so.

But she'd underestimated the threat against her. Even with the severed wire taunting her, she rebelled against the thought that someone would be so determined to target her. "Do you think someone damaged the wire on purpose?"

"They left just enough to permit us to take off, but with so little hanging on that it was bound to break sooner or later."

"Later enough that we'd be too far gone to catch who did it." Ginny finished his thought.

"And high enough in the sky—" Ben met her eyes and swallowed.

Ginny felt the clenching pain tighten around her heart. "High enough we'd probably never reach the ground alive."

FOUR

"What are we going to do now?" Ginny's round blue eyes were full of trust as she looked up at him.

Ben didn't want to break it to her, but he didn't have any easy answers. Sure, he had his Air Force training to guide him, but there was no simple solution that would whisk them out of the storm or the uninhabited region where they'd landed. "Let's see if we can get help." He reached inside the cabin for his backpack and pulled out his cell phone.

"I've got no connection." Fat drops of rain began to spatter down as the wind pushed the storm to breaking above them. Ben pulled Ginny a little closer under the makeshift cover of the up-tilted wing.

She looked over his shoulder and made a face at the screen.

"This is the problem with ninety-seven-percent coverage," he muttered, close enough to her ear that she could hear him clearly in spite of the wind. "The places where there aren't any people are the places where there isn't any coverage."

"Three percent of the country is still a lot of miles," Ginny agreed, matching his cynical tone. "I wish my satellite phone hadn't been destroyed in the fire. All the girls carry one. Maybe I should have asked to borrow someone else's." Regret filled Ginny's features. "And the radio won't work with the power wire severed. Do you think we can splice it back together?"

Ben had enough experience with plane engines to know better than to try it. "Not without risking greater damage to the electrical system. We should leave the engine alone until we can fix it properly. Otherwise we'll only make matters worse." He wished he had more positive news for her. "I'm going to head up the hill and try to find high ground. Maybe I'll be able to see a farmhouse or something."

"Good luck seeing anything in all this flying sand." Ginny's hand tightened on his sleeve. "Do you want me to stay here?"

Ben sensed the alarm that undergirded her words. She didn't want to be left alone with the plane—which was still unstable, even though he doubted it would explode now that several minutes had passed since they'd landed. But at the same time, he was reluctant to drag her through the rain and the storm. She'd only get soaking wet.

"You can wait inside the plane. I'll be right back," he promised her, eager to see what he could see before the rain got any worse. So far it was only spattering, but from the look of the dark clouds above them, it would progress to drenching in short order.

Ginny climbed back inside the tiny cabin and Ben bounded up the nearest hill. The rounded top wasn't all that high, but neither were the domes of the nearby hills. He had a pretty good view in spite of the rain. But there wasn't any sign of shelter or civilization as far as he could see in any direction.

The hope that shone on Ginny's face when he climbed inside the plane made him wish he had better news for her.

"Could you see anything?"

"Not in this rain. Maybe once the storm clears. In the meantime, the plane will keep us dry, and with the way the rain is starting to come down I don't think we need to worry about fire."

"That's reassuring." Ginny's smile looked forced, and she quickly turned her face away to look out the window. The pounding rain was coming down in buckets now.

Ben hesitated in the doorway. He had the door closed behind him to keep out the rain, but Ginny was sitting on the rear bench seat. Given the tilted-sideways angle at which the plane had come to rest, the front bucket seat didn't offer much of a spot to perch, especially not for his large frame.

But he wasn't about to ask Ginny to move. "Does this seat recline?" He reached for the front seat.

"What? Oh." Ginny sniffled and he realized she was fighting back tears. The situation was catching up with her. He hadn't wanted that to happen.

She gulped a breath. "You're not going to fit up there, I'm afraid." She struggled to her feet against the awkward tilt of the cabin. "Sorry, I wasn't thinking. How rude of me. I'll sit in the pilot's seat."

"I don't know if you can—" he started to protest, but she'd leapt to her feet and was already trying to squeeze past him in the confining space.

"Sorry. Excuse me," she apologized softly, not making eye contact as she grasped his bicep for balance on her way to the front. One final lunge landed her rump on the ridge of the sideways seat. "You can have the back seat."

Knowing there was no way Ginny could possibly be comfortable in such an awkward spot, Ben offered, "I can stay outside. The wings make good enough cover."

Ginny looked out the window, which streamed with

falling rain, and then back up at where he hovered indecisively between the door and the rear bench seat. "You've got to be kidding me. You'll get soaked." She shuffled around on her precarious perch. "Really, I'm fine here. You can sit in the back seat."

"It's your plane—"

"Sit!" Ginny cut off his protests in a commanding tone.

Ben sat. He felt like a caged bear in the tiny cockpit, and all the more so because he seemed to be failing in his attempts to keep Ginny safe.

Ginny had so far had her life threatened three times since his arrival in Wyoming the day before. Bobby Burbank was behind bars, but whoever had torched the trailer and severed the wire in the plane's engine was still out there somewhere. And as long as his identity remained a secret, Ginny's stalker would continue to have the upper hand.

"Who do you think," Ben started slowly and broke off. He cleared his throat. "Who might have tampered with the plane?"

Ginny put her hands up in a hopeless shrug. "I can't imagine. Maybe that Bobby Burbank fellow has an accomplice."

"That's possible," Ben acknowledged. "But he seemed to be a classic stalker, and stalkers tend to work alone. I wonder if you know of anyone close to you who might have a motive to get you out of the picture."

"Someone close to me?" Ginny looked hurt by his suggestion. "You mean, someone else from the stunt team? The Dare Divas flying troupe is like a family. None of us would hurt any of the others. It had to be someone on the outside. Besides, who says they're targeting me? All the Dare Divas have had problems."

A growl of protest rose in Ben's throat as he struggled to keep from arguing with Ginny. Not only did he fear that the Dare Divas' troubles centered around her, but as long as she disregarded an entire group of likely suspects simply on the grounds that she trusted them, she'd continue to put herself in danger. But how could he make her see that without making her more upset?

Forcing a casual tone into his voice, he probed further. "There isn't anyone who's acted jealous of you, who's been upset with you for any reason? You can't tell me everyone gets along all the time."

Ginny shifted on her perch. "Sure, we have our arguments from time to time. We've had disagreements about costumes and routines, but little things. Not the kind of thing you try to kill someone over."

"Nobody's jealous of you? Your face is on all the posters—you're the spokesperson on the commercials and radio spots. None of the other girls are envious of your position?"

"If they are, they haven't said anything." Ginny shook her head. "I know how it might look from the outside, but we support each other. There isn't a girl on that team I haven't trained at some point. I was one of the first pilots Doug and Ron hired. The Dare Divas Barnstorming Troupe wouldn't be the success we are today if it wasn't for all the hard work I put in, and I think the girls appreciate that. Everybody on the crew knows it, too. Where would they be if I wasn't around any more?"

Ben crossed his arms over his chest, thinking hard about what Ginny said. "Do you think it might be a competitor, then? Someone on the outside who might benefit from your downfall?"

"A competitor?" Ginny laughed. "Who? Do you know of any other all-female stunt-flying troupes that operate in our distinct niche? Or any other stunt fliers who perform on a similar circuit? We're unique."

"Fine," Ben felt his hands knotting with tension. "Nobody would have any reason to try to kill you, then. So those gunshots came out of nowhere and the mechanical troubles you've been having are just coincidences."

"I'm not saying that—"

"Then someone has to have a motive," Ben snapped back. "I'm not suggesting people just to hurt your feelings. I'm trying to sort this out in order to save your life."

"If I knew who was doing it I'd have said something by now," Ginny almost shouted. "Do you think I don't want this person caught? Of course I do." She shifted again on the edge of the crooked seat, clearly uncomfortable. "For all I know, *you're* behind it."

Ben's head snapped up and he tried to read her face, to tell if she was serious or just getting defensive. "Ginny." He softened his tone.

But she was quick to defend her accusation. "Sure— why not you, Ben? You could have set the fire last night, you were the one person with the greatest opportunity to tamper with the plane."

"Why would I tamper with a plane I was going to be riding in? Am I suicidal, too?"

"I don't know." She hopped off her seat and flexed her knees as though they'd finally had enough of their ridiculous perch. "If we can't rule anybody out, then I'm not going to rule you out, either."

"Good." Ben settled back. "Don't rule me out, or anyone else who might have had access to the plane this morning."

Ginny shifted her weight from one foot to the other, trying to restore circulation to her feet—sitting sideways on the edge of the pilot's seat had cut off blood flow. She really didn't like the spot she was in. The storm outside had grown furious, somebody was obviously out to kill her and Ben was taking up the whole back seat.

If it had been her brother sitting back there, or her grandfather or even one of the Dare Divas crew, she wouldn't have thought twice about squeezing in next to him. But the man in the back of the plane was a little too good-looking and a little too much of a stranger for her to feel comfortable sharing such close quarters with him, storm or no storm.

Besides, her suggestion that he might have been behind the attacks wasn't as absurd as he'd tried to make it sound. Though she felt like she could trust him, and he had only been gentle and helpful so far, Ginny also trusted everyone else who'd had access to the plane that morning. But *someone* was trying to kill her. So it wasn't wise for her to trust anyone at the moment.

"It's not as though you have no motive," Ginny reminded Ben as she tried to find a comfortable spot with her back pressed against the pilot's seat back. But the space was still too cramped and the move only brought her closer to Ben.

"What would my motive be?" Ben asked, amusement sparkling behind the anger in his eyes.

"Well, there's that old family feud, you know—between the McCutcheons and the McAlisters. Our grandfathers ran rival airstrips, and didn't your family blame mine when your grandfather's plane went down years ago?"

"I don't think there was ever anything more than conjecture to link your family to that accident." Ben scowled a little and looked thoughtful. "Grandpa was dusting crops with quite a bit of cold medicine in his system—that's what I was told caused the crash. Anyway, since Cutch and Elise got back together, the old feud was put to rest. So there goes your theory."

Ginny wasn't nearly so quick to let the matter drop. She'd heard enough about the stupid feud growing up; Ben couldn't possibly dismiss the whole thing that easily. "So Cutch and Elise get along now, but what about you? Don't you still resent the McCutcheons? I thought your Uncle Bill hated my family."

Ben's eyes twinkled, and Ginny couldn't help wondering why. "When you get back to Holyoake," he said suggestively, "you'll find my Uncle Bill has softened considerably toward the McCutcheons."

His words sent an odd little shiver down Ginny's spine, and she wondered whether the upward bend of his lips came from a smile or a smirk. "What do you mean by that?" She absently lifted one foot behind her in an attempt to stretch the last cramp from her legs.

"Have you talked to your mother lately?"

"Sure, on the phone, but she didn't mention anything about any McAlisters except Elise."

Now the smirk on Ben's face was certainly a full-blown smile. "You'll have to ask her about it, then."

Distracted by the dimple that appeared on Ben's cheek as he grinned up at her, and wondering what on earth his vague insinuations about her mother might mean, Ginny forgot that she was standing on one leg in the awkwardly-tilted plane. As she wobbled forward and lost her balance, she flung her arms out in an attempt to catch herself.

Ben leapt up and caught her easily, settling her gently beside him on the rear bench seat. "Why don't you just sit back here?"

Ginny had plenty of reasons why she didn't want to sit back there with Ben—mostly because he was good-looking and did funny things to her heart. But she wasn't about to confess any of that, so she closed her eyes against the embarrassment she'd just experienced and the whole horrible situation surrounding them. "Fine."

"You look exhausted. Maybe you can rest."

Since it gave her an excuse not to have to open her eyes, look at him and risk another funny leap from her heart, Ginny agreed. "I *am* tired. That stupid fire last night." She yawned at the reminder of all the sleep she'd lost out on.

"Try to get some rest. Maybe by the time you wake up, the storm will be over and we can get out of here."

"Uh-huh," she agreed, the weight of her eyelids feeling like a heavy blanket after the nearly sleepless night she'd been through. "That would be nice." Her heart pinched inside her, the same fear-fueled stress that had pained her since Kristy's accident, and Ginny shifted her body in hopes that might relieve some of the pain.

Her cheek met brushed cotton and she peeked her eyes open just enough to see the loden color of Ben's chambray shirt. Maybe she should try to move away from him, but there really wasn't anywhere else she could go, and she'd finally found a comfortable spot. So what if his shoulder was beneath her cheek? She was too tired to care.

And it *was* a very nice shoulder.

Pulling in a deep breath as slumber crept closer, she picked up Ben's masculine scent and wondered if she'd be crazy to let herself trust the man as much as she wanted to. But he'd saved her from the fire the night before, and his point about sabotaging the airplane was a good one—he wouldn't be crazy enough to endanger a flight he was on. Besides, if he'd wanted to hurt her, he'd had plenty of other opportunities already.

In her heart of hearts, Ginny knew Ben was trustworthy. But her heart also told her things about this man that made her feel mighty uncomfortable. She respected him.

She admired him. They had a lot in common—like a love for flying and their Holyoake roots. He'd be an easy guy to fall for if she was in the market for a man.

But she absolutely wasn't looking. No, she'd figured out soon enough after her stunt-flying gig made her a minor celebrity that a lot of the guys who expressed interest in her were only hoping to catch a moment in the limelight. She'd quickly gotten very picky about whom she would see romantically. When she'd met Kevin four years before, his sincerity had finally convinced her that he wasn't just with her in hopes of getting his picture in the paper.

She'd had real feelings for Kevin. Unfortunately, her flying schedule and the fame that came with it had been too much for their relationship. She and Kevin had tried to make things work, but Kevin had finally admitted he couldn't compete with her job. He wanted a woman with both feet on the ground. And she loved flying too much to give it up. She couldn't be with a man who wanted to clip her wings.

So she'd made up her mind: Until she was ready to give up flying and commit herself to settling down with a man, she wasn't even going to consider a relationship.

Besides, wasn't Ben considerably older than she was? He'd joined the Air Force right out of high school, and she'd been, what, a second grader at the time? The man had to have a decade on her, maybe more. So even if she was looking, which she most definitely wasn't, Ben was beyond consideration, anyway.

He had a nice shoulder to lean on, that was all. And as soon as it stopped raining and they got home to Holyoake, she'd be sure to put some distance between them. Because if her guess was right, and whoever was targeting the troupe had a special grudge against her, then the attacker wasn't going to give up just because she'd flown the coop. And the last thing she wanted to do was let a nice guy like Ben get caught in the crossfire.

The rain had stopped. Ben knew they still had a few hours of daylight ahead of them, so he wasn't in a hurry to leave. He certainly wasn't going to awaken the sleeping beauty who rested in his arms. She'd had enough stress to deal with lately and could obviously use the sleep after hardly getting any the night before. If that meant he got to spend a little longer admiring her rosebud lips or the adorable smattering of freckles that graced her face, he wasn't going to complain.

Besides, sitting still gave him quiet time to puzzle over who might have sabotaged the plane, and who might have lit the fire under Ginny's trailer the night before. He assumed both crimes had been perpetrated by the same person, or at least people working together. Ginny's insistence on the innocence of her friends didn't convince him for a minute, either. Their suspect was most likely someone who knew Ginny—probably someone who knew her well, who had access to her schedule and knew when would be the best time to strike.

As soon as they reached Holyoake, Ben was going to give his younger brother Tyler a call. Tyler had served in the Air Force as well, but had left several years before to work for a private investigation firm. He could do background checks on any names Ben gave him. If anyone had a record, Tyler would find it.

But a background in crime wasn't necessarily a prerequisite for attempted murder. Obviously their suspect was determined—not only had there been several attempts on Ginny's life, but they seemed to be getting more frequent, and more desperate. Such a person probably had a deepseated reason for wanting Ginny dead. And such a depth of passion was most likely to be found among those who had regular contact with Ginny.

Though he knew the barnstorming beauty didn't like the idea, Ben still thought it highly likely that whoever was out to kill her was someone who was already close to her. Obviously his first attempt to discuss the issue had been a bust. Regardless of whether she wanted to have the conversation, Ben was determined to discuss the issue with Ginny again.

In spite of all the unknowns surrounding the attempts on Ginny's life, one thing was perfectly certain: whoever was after her meant business. It might only be a matter of time before the would-be killer found his target. Ben *had* to catch whoever it was before anything happened to Ginny. He couldn't bear the idea that the killer might succeed.

FIVE

Ginny breathed in deeply, her sleep-slurred mind skimming over sunny thoughts like a plane gliding through wisps of cloud. She'd had a happy dream, for once. No memory of it remained to hint at what it had been about, but she was certain it had been a happy one. And she felt well-rested, too. That hadn't happened in some time.

And, she realized as she sucked in another deep breath without feeling the usual accompanying pinch of pain, her heart didn't hurt anymore.

Her heart didn't hurt anymore?

The shock of it pulled her consciousness a little higher out of the deep well of sleep, and she focused on drawing in another deep breath.

No pinch near her lungs. No twinge of pain with each heartbeat. No erratic heartbeat at all. She almost felt at peace. Now how had that happened?

Puzzled right out of her restful state, Ginny sucked in another painless breath and snuggled a little deeper into her pillow. Except it wasn't a pillow underneath her cheek at all, she realized. It was a chambray shirt.

Ginny sat bolt upright and nearly knocked her head against the inside wall of the plane. Just before her head met the wall, Ben's hand darted between the two, and she thunked her noggin against his palm instead.

"Did I hurt you?" she gasped.

"Hardly." He smiled down at her.

There was that troublesome dimple again.

"What time is it?" Blue sky filled the upward-tilted window as she looked around. "It stopped raining?"

"Yup. We should get going," Ben suggested. He shifted sideways, obviously waiting for her to stand so he could follow her out of the plane.

"Get going?" Ginny felt irritated by her unwanted attraction to the man. "What do you mean? Isn't the first rule of wilderness crashes to always stay with the plane?"

Ben leaned a little closer to her. "Who do you think would be first to find us? The only person who has reason to believe we may be out here is the person who tampered with the plane. No one else would be looking for us yet."

His sudden nearness only made her feel flustered, but she quickly realized his argument was a valid one. As she hurried to disembark, she tried to tell herself not to allow him to affect her. The only reason she felt so self-conscious was because she felt an unwelcome smidgen of attraction toward Ben. But he couldn't possibly guess at her feelings unless she gave herself away by acting embarrassed.

Determined to keep her feelings a secret, she schooled her expression and hopped out of the plane, hoping that if her cheeks were noticeably red, Ben would just attribute it to the fact that she'd been asleep.

Grabbing her backpack, she started trudging up the nearest hill.

"Where are you headed?" Ben stood, unmoving, by the door of the plane.

"Uphill." She fumbled for words, reminding herself that she had no reason to be embarrassed. None that she could let on to Ben about, anyway. "So I can see which direction we should head."

"Do you want your water bottle?" Ben asked.

Ginny stopped. "Oh. Good idea." Reluctantly she retraced her steps back to the plane and spent a few moments with Ben deciding what they ought to bring and how they ought to leave the plane. She made it a point not to look into his green-and-brown mottled eyes.

"Okay, let's head out," she declared finally, and turned to head up the hill.

Ben's hand settled on her shoulder, effectively holding her back.

"What?" she asked impatiently.

"You seem a little scattered." Ben stepped around her side and settled his other hand on her opposite shoulder. "Maybe you should take a moment to make sure you're fully awake."

"Okay." Her voice wavered as she risked a glance up into his face. Not a good idea. Had the man gotten even handsomer while she wasn't looking? He'd started to sprout a bit of five o'clock shadow that made him look even more rugged and which, if anything, enhanced that mischievous dimple.

"Do you mind if I pray?" Ben asked. "I should have offered to pray before we took off this morning, but it's never too late."

In Ginny's well-practiced experience, prayer didn't help anything. But it would give her an excuse to close her eyes while she collected her thoughts. "Go for it."

"Dear Lord," Ben began earnestly, "we ask for Your protection and guidance. Thank You so much for protecting Ginny over these last few weeks, and thank You especially for giving us a safe landing this morning. Right now we don't know what to do, or which way to go, but we know that You know the way, Lord. Lead us safely back home. We pray in Jesus' name, Amen."

Ginny felt a treacherous tear slip from the corner of her eye, and she gave a sniffle in spite of herself. She didn't really believe Ben's prayer would change anything, but she missed believing. And there was a tiny part of her heart that sincerely wished that God was listening and would help them. But she'd learned otherwise the hard way.

"Hey." Ben's open palm swept across her cheek, brushing away the tear. "It's going to be okay."

"Uh-huh," Ginny gulped a breath and willed away the emotion that threatened to overwhelm her. "We should get going."

They climbed the hill side by side. To Ginny's disappointment, all she could see from the top was green scrubby hills in every direction. There weren't even any trees, and certainly no buildings or cell phone towers. Small, hardy wildflowers tipped their heads in the breeze, and a meadowlark perched on a particularly tall frond of prairie grass, trilling its song and cocking its head at them curiously. If she hadn't been lost in the hills, she might have found the setting charming. As it was, the endless rolling green made her stomach churn.

"Which way?" she asked Ben, hoping he might have some clue of their position.

"Do you have any idea where we are?" His question did little to buoy her hopes.

"Nebraska?" She wasn't even completely certain of that much, though the terrain seemed to fit the state.

"Most of Nebraska's population lives in the eastern part of the state."

"So we should head east?" Ginny wondered if they weren't about to embark on an interstate trek.

"It's as good a direction as any."

They trudged on in silence. After rounding the first couple of hills, Ginny quickly came to resent the super-soft sandy soil that made her feet sink and gave her calves an extra workout. It was worse than jogging on the beach. There were sandburs everywhere, and her fingertips soon burned from prying the prickly barbs from her socks. To make matters worse, all the extra foot-shifting caused the sneakers she wore to rub on the back of her heels. She could feel blisters forming.

They topped a particularly high hill and Ginny paused to take a drink from her water bottle. "Can you see anything?"

"Cows."

"Cows are a good sign. Cows mean farmers, right?"

"Somewhere." Ben sounded unconvinced.

Ginny screwed the cap tightly back in place. "Can you see any roads?" She couldn't see any, but she hoped that from the vantage point of his extra five inches of height Ben might be able to see a little farther than she could.

"Not yet."

"Let's head toward the cows, then." At the very least, even if they didn't find a farmstead, she hoped to hit a road, where hopefully walking wouldn't grate her ankles so badly. The shoes she'd borrowed after the fire were far from a perfect fit. Even if they didn't find a road, maybe they'd come down into a valley that harbored some tree cover. Anything to keep them from wandering through the wide-open dunes, where whoever was out to kill her could easily find them and pick them off from the sky.

Her heart pinched at the thought, and she quickly tried to chase it from her mind. As Ben took off down the side of the hill, Ginny decided she needed a conversation to distract her from her anxious thoughts. "I could really go for a big, juicy cheeseburger right now."

"Is that why you wanted to head toward the cattle?" Ben's voice held a distinct teasing tone, and when Ginny looked up and caught his eye, his smirk was back, and so was his dimple.

She chuckled at his suggestion. "Tell you what, I'll milk a cow and make us some cheese. You get the beef, okay?"

Her suggestion sounded absurd to her ears, and Ben must have found the image humorous as well, because he threw his head back and laughed.

She definitely preferred laughing with Ben over trudging in silence. It was almost enough to take her mind off her worries. They joked their way over several more hilltops before a prairie dog tunnel gave way under Ginny's foot, yanking her ankle harshly to the side.

Ben was still chuckling over something she'd said, but at her frightened yelp he immediately got his arm under her and half caught her before she hit the ground, steadying her as she rose slowly to an upright position.

"Did you sprain it?" Concern shone in his eyes.

Much as she wanted to deny any pain, Ginny couldn't put any weight on the foot without wincing. "Just give me a second." When she tried to point her toes, tears sprang to her eyes.

"Let me take a look at that." Ben already had his arm under hers, and he settled her back against the hill, quickly setting to work plucking sandburs from her shoelaces before untying them.

Ginny watched, mystified by this burly man whose touch could be so gentle. He soon got the laces undone and tugged the shoe from her foot.

"Ahh!" Sympathetic pain filled his voice when he revealed the burst blisters on Ginny's heel.

She'd suspected her feet might be in such condition,

but she hadn't wanted to say anything. The last thing she'd wanted to do was give them a reason to stop. No matter how enjoyable it had been to laugh and joke with Ben, she hadn't forgotten that a murderer was after her. The wide-open sand hills offered no cover. All anyone had to do was find her downed plane and follow their footprints east.

And now she wouldn't even be able to run away. Already her ankle had begun to swell.

"Why didn't you tell me you were getting blisters?" Ben chided her.

"I didn't want to slow us down." Her defense sounded feeble, especially since she knew she was really going to delay them now.

Ben pulled a packet of Band-Aids from his backpack. "I suppose your other heel is just as bad."

"I suppose," Ginny echoed softly, sniffling as she got to work plucking the sandburs from the laces of her other shoe. She was fairly certain the other foot was actually worse, but Ben would find that out soon enough.

"These aren't your shoes, are they?" Ben asked.

"The fire destroyed mine," Ginny reminded him. "The girls rounded these up for me. I think these were Veronica's shoes. She's the only girl whose feet are as big as mine."

"That's part of your problem. Your feet aren't used to them, and they look like they're a tad too big. I wish I'd realized..." His words dropped off as he shook his head regretfully.

While Ben took care of her raw blisters, Ginny tried to sniff back the frightened tears that welled in her eyes. They were in the middle of nowhere. Though they'd survived the plane crash, whoever had cut that engine wire had still won. She couldn't imagine how she'd ever get out of the endless sand hills alive. At the rate she was going, the murderer wouldn't even have to catch up with them.

She'd already managed to injure herself; it would only be a matter of time before they ran out of water. And the June day hadn't cooled, in spite of the sinking sun.

Ben finished work on her blistered heels and Ginny pulled her shoes back on, loosening the laces considerably to get the left shoe on, since the swelling from her ankle had already spread down her foot. She sniffled again, but this time a tear escaped.

"Hey, kiddo, none of that," Ben chided her. "You'll wash off your sunblock. Don't redheads have to be careful about that sort of thing?"

"It's coming on evening," she reminded him, "past peak sunburn time." She got her laces retied and Ben offered her a hand, pulling her to standing before dropping to his knees.

"What?"

"Climb on my back."

"You're *not* going to carry me."

"Yes, I am." He looked up at her from the vantage point of his knees, and squinted against the sinking sun that burned behind her. "You can't walk, and I'm certainly not going to leave you out here."

Nor did Ginny want to be left, even if she thought there was some hope Ben might be able to reach help and come back for her, which she didn't. The idea of being alone in the wilderness was almost as frightening as her growing attraction for the man who offered to carry her.

"You can't carry me," she protested again, though her voice lacked conviction, even to her own ears.

"Hurry up and climb on. We're wasting time."

Against her better judgment, Ginny flopped onto Ben's back and wrapped her arms around his shoulders. He hoisted her up effortlessly.

"Let me know if you get tired." She tried not to think

about the strong flex of his muscles as she clung to his shoulders. "Maybe my ankle will start to feel better after a little rest, and I'll be able to walk on it." Ginny knew the sprain was serious, but she hoped to muster up enough grit to walk on it anyway.

"That looked like a second-degree sprain from the way it was swelling. It probably won't feel better for a week."

Ginny didn't want to feel discouraged by Ben's prognosis. A sprained ankle was the least of her worries. She felt a rush of gratitude that Ben was with her and that he was willing to carry her. Though he was a strong man, she wasn't particularly light, not with her tall frame and both their backpacks.

After trudging over and around several more hills, she noticed Ben's pace began to slow.

"This next hill looks higher. Maybe we can see something from there," she suggested.

Ben obediently made the climb, though he didn't even so much as offer to tackle a cow as they passed the herd they'd seen from a distance. Was he losing his sense of humor? Ginny suspected he was probably just plain beat.

The top of the hill, as she'd hoped, offered a wide view of the surrounding countryside. Though the vista was a scenic one in its own way, the novelty of unending hills had long since worn off. She saw no sign of roads or trees anywhere.

Discouraged, she slid off Ben's sagging back, landing with most of her weight on her good foot and leaning against Ben for balance.

"I think we should take a breather."

"We should keep going." Ben sounded tired. "It's finally starting to cool off. The cool evening will be the best time for walking. We can rest when the sun comes up."

"You can't be serious. You're *not* carrying me any farther. You need a break."

Ben uncapped his water and took a sip. Ginny had noticed that he'd been rationing it. She'd tried doing the same, but her thirst demanded more. It was so hot out. And, she realized with another twinge of guilt, she'd expended quite a bit of moisture in her tears.

They needed a plan.

"We're going to need to find water." She pointed out. "Don't the cows have to have a water source?"

"I don't see a windmill."

"Neither do I." Ginny knew farmers in such remote areas still used traditional windmills to pump water for their herds. Surely the cows wouldn't wander far from a water source. But something as tall as a windmill should have been visible if it was in the area.

"There must be a stream nearby, or a pond," Ben theorized. "It's probably deep between the hills in a low-lying point. That's why we can't see it."

Ginny looked around them again, trying to think how they might find where the cows got their water. She knew the animals couldn't go long without it. "I know what we need to do." She grasped Ben's arm. "Let's circle back around by the cows and try to find their water source."

"You think we should start wandering in circles?" Ben looked skeptical. "Deliberately?"

"We're not going to get much farther without water. You said yourself the cows have to have a water source out here. We'll stay within sight of the herd."

"What if the herd moves?"

"If they move, won't they go closer to water?" She let out a frustrated sigh. "We need water. If I thought we'd find a road or a farmhouse soon, I'd head for that. But we're not going to find anything if we get too dehydrated to keep going."

And though she wasn't going to mention it to Ben, she hoped that by finding a water source such as a creek or pond, they might also find some bushes, maybe even a small tree—anything they could hide under. Surely whoever had damaged that wire would want to know if the damage had done the job. Ginny feared it would only be a matter of time before her would-be killer caught up to them. Even though they hadn't made their destination known, anyone could have watched which direction they'd flown off in. She wished she'd thought of taking an indirect route to throw off their pursuers, but it was too late for that now. Once again, she'd underestimated her adversary.

Ben's thoughtful pause indicated he was weighing her suggestion. "I don't know—"

"Why not?" Ginny couldn't understand why he was fighting her. The plan seemed perfectly sensible to her.

Ben's brown-green eyes settled on her, and for the first time, Ginny caught a glimpse of fear through the cracks in his armor. "We need to get out of these hills. I shouldn't have let you rest as long as I did. I didn't think it would take so long to get out of here. I'm sorry. I didn't think."

Closing her eyes against the reality of Ben's words and the closeness of his face to hers, Ginny took a deep breath and tried to come up with a plan. There had to be a way out of their situation.

A droning sound hummed faintly in the distance.

"What's that?" Her eyes popped back open. Was that an engine? "Are we near a road?"

Ben's eyes had grown wide as well. "It sounds like a plane." He looked up, then quickly around them as though he expected elusive cover to appear out of nowhere.

"There!" He pointed to a plane-shaped dot in the distance. It was still too far away to try to make out any markings, or even identify what kind of plane it was.

Pain shot back through Ginny's heart, fear-driven pain that made her lungs catch. Her killer was coming after her. She'd known they would.

"To the herd!" She squeezed Ben's arm. She couldn't run. He'd have to carry her.

"The cows?"

"It's the closest thing to cover we've got out here." She wasn't sure exactly how the cows would camouflage them—perhaps they could crouch in the shadow of an animal. She wished they could cling like burs to their undersides, but that was something that would happen in a cartoon, not in real life. In this remote area, the cattle surely weren't used to seeing humans very often—they had already demonstrated a tendency to move away from Ben and Ginny when they'd passed by before.

"If we go running at the cows, we could cause a stampede," Ben cautioned her.

"Good. That will provide distraction. Maybe the pilot will assume the plane caused the stampede." Already the drone of the motor buzzed more loudly above them. Ginny could see the plane flying low in the sky, and it appeared to be gliding slowly, like they weren't in any hurry. Like they were looking for someone.

"It's a better plan than anything I've got." Ben scooped her up into his arms and ran toward the herd. "At least the cow prints will help disguise our footprints."

He rounded the next hill and was panting hard by the time they closed in on the herd. As predicted, the sudden appearance of the six-foot-three-inch airman and his redheaded burden caused the nearest cow to startle and jump away.

Ben fell forward into the soft earth, shifting Ginny into the grass beside him as he went down. "Don't move." He panted into her ear.

"We need to get closer." She still felt completely exposed in the wide-open hills. The tallest of the knee-high grasses were still far too sparse to hide in.

"If we get any closer the cows will bolt. If the plane's flying high enough, we'll blend in like just another speck on the ground."

Ginny could hear the whine of the engine drawing closer. It sounded as though it might pass south of them, but if the plane's occupants had spotted her downed wingwalker, they would surely circle around again. And she was pretty sure the aircraft wasn't traveling so high that they'd look like a speck. They'd most likely look like Ben and Ginny, crouching in the grass like toddlers trying to hide by covering their eyes. That old trick didn't make two-year-olds disappear, and she was certain it wouldn't conceal them.

Fortunately the sun continued to droop lower in the sky. Already the day's light had begun to fade. If they could escape notice long enough, the sun would go down and so would their chances of being found, at least until morning.

"Lord, protect us under the shadow of Your wings. Shield us from our enemies." Ben's voice rumbled out a prayer beside her.

As his monotone muttering continued, the drone of the plane's engine began to fade. Was it passing by them? Ginny still had yet to get a decent look at the thing. Creeping her hand through the grass to where Ben's hand lay near her, she laced her fingers into his. Maybe she didn't really believe that God would answer his prayers, but she still found the words soothing. She was glad Ben still had hope, even if she didn't.

He turned his head and caught her eye between the grasses that separated them. "It's passing by," he whispered.

She smiled a hesitant smile. "Do you think it will see my plane?"

"Sounds like it's headed that way."

"Did it come from the east?"

"Hard to tell. They may have been circling." Ben squeezed her hand.

Ginny had participated in a few aerial searches over the years, volunteering her time when hikers got lost or bush pilots failed to return home. She remembered thinking then how vast the terrain could be, and how miniscule a missing person seemed in comparison. But that had been in mountainous areas with plenty of tree cover. Out here in the wide-open grasslands, the odds still seemed to be in favor of those with a bird's-eye view.

The sound of the engine, which had begun to fade, now buzzed louder again. "Are they headed back our way?" Ginny asked.

Ben nodded. "Let's try to get closer to the herd." He scooped her up and crept toward a gap between several grazing animals. Again he lowered her gently to the ground as the sound of the plane grew louder than it had before.

Ginny peeked past Ben's shoulder. He crouched above her, shielding her, whether from view or from anything that might be shot at them she wasn't sure, but she appreciated the cover he provided and the smaller target they made because of his efforts. She'd wrapped her arms around his shoulders to hold on while he carried her, and now she felt her fingers tighten their grip almost against her will.

"I can see the plane." She swallowed back her fear.

"Recognize it?"

"No." She scowled. Shouldn't she be able to recognize it, though? If her killer really was someone close to her, then it followed that the plane would be one that was housed among the Dare Divas fleet. "It's white with red stripes. A Cessna."

"Skyhawk?" Ben asked, twisting around to see.

"Looks like it." Ginny wished he'd stay still, but the man seemed determined to get a look at the plane.

Ben looked back down at her, this time his face so close she could feel his breath against her skin as he spoke. "Can you walk? Or try to hobble if I support your injured side?"

"I don't know." Ginny swallowed. "Why?"

"We've got to get to a road, and we need to hurry."

Ginny felt her eyes go wide.

Ben glanced up once more as the plane drew nearer. "I know that plane."

SIX

Ben wasn't sure who was piloting the plane, but he recognized his cousin Elise's Cessna Skyhawk. Relieved as he was that they'd flown so close, he still didn't want the pilot to try to land on the soft hilly soil. The last thing they needed was to crash-land two planes. That would only put more people in danger. There *had* to be a road somewhere.

As the plane drew nearer, Ben jumped up, grabbed his bright-red backpack and waved it in the air.

Ginny scrambled up after him. "What are you doing? Who is it?"

"That's Elise's plane. They must have come looking for us."

"Are you sure?" Ginny's expression said she wanted to err on the side of caution.

But all Ben's frantic flagging had caught the pilot's attention. The peppermint-striped plane circled low. Through the down-turned window Ben recognized a familiar grin.

"That's my little brother, Tyler." Ben waved back, trying to communicate with his brother by gesturing to ask if he could see a road. Tyler only shrugged as the plane skimmed through the air past them, swooping up higher again.

Ben turned to Ginny. "We've got to find a place for him to land. He won't have any better luck on these sand hills than you did." Even if Tyler managed to land his plane without rolling it, he'd never get back off the ground. The sand was simply too soft and the hills too frequent.

"Get to the top of the hill." Ginny pulled him after her as she hobbled forward, half hopping on her good foot.

"We couldn't see a road from the last hill." Ben reminded her, wrapping an arm around her waist to prop up her injured side.

Ginny hopped resolutely, a determined expression on her freckled face. "We don't need a road."

"Tyler doesn't dare land on this sand. You're the better pilot and you couldn't do it."

"He doesn't need to *land*. He just needs to fly low and slow."

A sickening feeling began to churn in Ben's stomach.

Ginny cast a grin up at him. "Have you ever seen one of my air shows?"

"I've seen several." The churning sensation grew more ominous.

"Has Tyler seen one?" Ginny's smile grew brighter.

"A couple." Ben had dragged his brother along more than once so he could show off their "long-lost relative" Ginger McAlister. Of course, Ben hadn't known then who Ginger really was. He'd just been tickled that they shared a last name, and thought she was the most fantastic female with four wings.

"Excellent. Then he should be able to figure out what to do."

Ben knew exactly what Ginny was getting at. He'd seen the stunt plenty of times—and been wowed by the death-defying tricks the Dare Divas performed. Tricks he'd never dream of attempting. "Are you thinking about that human pyramid, where the acrobats grab the plane and climb aboard as it swoops low over them?"

"That's the one."

"You're insane."

"The term is 'death-defying'," Ginny corrected him, her smile unwavering. "And don't worry, I'm not going to ask you to form another pyramid on top of the flying plane like the girls do in the shows."

"That's a relief." Ben rolled his eyes. He'd never understood women and now sincerely wished he knew how to talk some sense into Ginny. But the way her eyes twinkled with a mixture of determination and relief, he doubted she'd listen to him no matter what he said.

"Now—" Ginny looked at the plane, scrutinizing the underside of the plane that tilted toward them as Tyler brought the Cessna around in a circle "—you're going to need to grab a fender, then pull yourself up. The trickiest part will be getting a tight hold as the plane glides by so you don't immediately fall off." She turned her attention back to Ben. "Do you want to go first or do you want me to show you how it's done?"

Ben had to look away from the bright-eyed young woman. He focused his attention on the plane that his brother flew in a wide arc through the evening sky above them. Ginny looked so determined, but he feared for her safety. She was right: It was a death-defying stunt they were about to perform. Even a single misstep could spell disaster. His brother had never before piloted a plane that was picking up acrobats from a hilltop. Ben had certainly never climbed aboard a flying Cessna from the ground.

And, he realized as he looked back down at Ginny, likely neither had she. "You're a pilot," he stated aloud. "Have you ever been part of the pyramid before?"

Ginny blushed red under cheeks that, in spite of her

sunblock, had picked up some extra color during their jaunt through the desert. "I've been part of this act hundreds of times."

"As the pilot."

She looked down.

Ben's heart went out to her. He knew her feet and ankle had to be killing her, and even if Tyler could spot a road for them and point them in the right direction, they'd still have a long trek ahead of them to get there. Night would be falling soon. And there was still every likelihood that whoever had sabotaged the plane could catch up to them at any moment—and would have no trouble finding them with Tyler circling overhead like a beacon.

Placing his hand lightly on her shoulder, Ben waited for Ginny to look up and meet his eyes before he said, "I just don't want you to get hurt. You're already injured and exhausted. Do you really think we can do this?"

Ginny looked up to where Tyler flew the Cessna near enough that the questioning expression on his face was clearly visible through the window. "I really think this is our best shot for getting out of here alive." She spoke evenly, a guileless expression on her face.

Ben took a deep breath and shook his head. "I was afraid of that."

"Why?"

"I was hoping for an excuse not to try it."

Ginny grinned at his admission. "You scared, McAlister?"

"Not if you're not—" he puffed his chest out "—McAlister."

He glanced down at her again and felt the air knocked from his lungs by the dazzling smile she returned him. Sucking in a breath, he focused on the plane. By now his brother was circling with just enough speed to keep the plane aloft. Perfect.

"We need to signal to Tyler to get low enough for us to grab on." Ginny squinted against the dying sun as Tyler swooped past again.

"How about if I put you up on my shoulders? That should give him an idea of what we're up to, and then you can show me how it's done." He didn't want her putting any weight on her bad ankle while she tried to catch the slow-gliding plane.

Ginny only hesitated a moment. "Okay." They agreed to leave their backpacks on the ground, since they had to return to the sand hills for Ginny's plane later and neither of them had anything too important in the packs anyway. By the time Tyler swooped past again, Ginny was balanced precariously on Ben's shoulders, her arms in the air, while Ben gripped her lower legs to stabilize her.

"Does he know how low to fly?" Ginny shouted as the drone of the approaching motor threatened to drown out her voice.

"He's an Air Force pilot," Ben shouted back. "And don't forget, he's taken his turn crop dusting at home." He watched with a twinge of pride as his brother brought the plane down in a low, easy swoop. Tyler was smart. He'd clearly figured out what they were about to attempt. And if Cutch had let on to the other McAlisters about Ginny's true identity, then Tyler likely had no reservations about trying the stunt. Of course, he wasn't the one who was going to be dangling from the landing gear.

Ben's leg muscles flexed as he stood ready to align himself with the approaching slow-moving plane.

"Try to get me on the passenger side," Ginny shouted down at him as the Cessna glided closer.

He felt Ginny's feet leave his shoulders as she grasped

the passing landing gear. A moment later her feet kicked the air in front of his face and he tried to push her back up.

She came down in a tangle, bowling him over into the sandy hillside.

"Ouch!" He barked as pain speared through his arm.

"Did I hurt you?"

"Not you." Ben rolled away from the offending barbs. "I landed on a cactus." He looked down at the mashed succulent, and winced as Ginny's agile fingers began plucking the stubborn spines from his bicep through his shirtsleeve.

"Sorry. I almost had it. My hands slipped. You should have jumped clear."

"And let *you* land on the cactus? From ten feet in the air?"

"Now you're injured." She bit her lip and looked up at him.

Ben heard the waver in her voice, and the exhaustion and fear that was so close to breaking through the surface. She was trying *so* hard.

"Don't worry about my arm. Let's give it another go. Tyler's coming around again. You'll get it this time." He looked down at her and watched doubt flit across her features. "I'll run under the plane as you're grabbing on. Don't try to put your weight into it until you've got a tight hold."

The wisdom in his words must have resonated with her, because she nodded solemnly. "There's a ladder step halfway up the wheel brace. If I can get one hand on that, I'll be able to pull my legs up on the fender. Then it's just a matter of getting the door open."

Ben grinned, thanking God that Ginny wasn't beaten yet. She had more spunk than a lot of the young guys he'd worked with in the Air Force, and that was saying something. The plane circled around, turning back toward them.

"Do you want up on my shoulders again?"

"Please." Ginny looked appreciative. "I can't run under the plane on my own. Not on this ankle."

Ben dropped to a crouch so she could climb on his shoulders, then raised up slowly once she was steady above him. He had a better idea of what to expect this time. The sound of the plane's motor rose to a roar as it came near them. Focusing all his attention on the landing gear that protruded from the underside of the approaching plane, Ben sprang into action the instant he heard Ginny's hands slap against the metal wheel hubs. He trotted along in the direction the slow-gliding plane flew, keeping Ginny steady until he felt her weight leave his shoulders completely.

He looked up and grinned when he saw that she had both hands solidly wrapped around the leg of the landing gear, and had one knee hooked over the fender as well.

Then he caught a movement in the distance and his optimism shattered. Another plane was swiftly moving in on them. This time, from the west. The distinctive red dart design and Dare Divas logo splashed across the side told him exactly where it had come from. But who was flying it? And what was their intention?

Bright-red glare from the setting sun completely obscured any visibility of the plane's interior, and the intense reflection on the windshield forced him to turn his head away before he could see who was at the controls. The plane was a concern, but not nearly as important as the situation Ginny was in. Ben squinted in her direction and was relieved to see her standing with her good foot on the ladder step, one hand gripping the open door and most of her upper body inside the plane.

"Keep it low and slow, Tyler," Ben murmured as he watched Ginny muscle her way inside the plane. "Lord, help her," he prayed as she got one hip inside the cabin and shifted around to pull the rest of her body in. For a moment she faced him with a look of concentration and satisfaction on her face.

His attention was so focused on Ginny's progress, he forgot about the other plane screaming down at him until Ginny's eyes widened and she gestured with her head, shouting something he couldn't begin to hear. He spun around to see the propeller of the approaching plane chopping through the air ten feet behind him, its landing gear all but skimming the grass as it tried to plow him down.

Ben hit the ground and screamed as his knee met another cactus. Well, that answered his question about what the red dart was up to. He winced as he eased himself into a sitting position, checking to be sure he didn't end up on another cactus.

Elise's Cessna curved back toward him. He could see Ginny through the window, urging him up.

The other plane came around in a fast arc. Mooing protests filled the air as the herd of cattle scattered all around him. They hadn't minded the slow-gliding Cessna, but the angry red stunt plane presented a threat even the cattle could recognize.

Ben's heart sank. How was he supposed to get aboard the Cessna? Tyler didn't dare slow down again or the red dart would be upon them.

Ginny opened the door as Tyler skimmed the air above him. "Ben, get up! Hurry!"

"No!" He shouted over her, realizing quickly what needed to happen. "Tell Tyler to take you home. I'll be fine!" He wasn't sure if she could hear him, but he shouted at the top of his lungs, waved her off, pointed homeward and hoped she'd get the idea. All he cared about was getting her back to Holyoake safely. If that meant he had to spend the night in the desert, it would be a small price to pay.

The red dart sped back around toward him. For a moment he feared the plane was going to try to smash into Ginny and Tyler, but he realized that would be a suicide mission. The other pilot must have reached the same conclusion, because the plane angled toward Ben, skimming close to the hill again, and sending what remained of the herd of cattle running in bovine terror through the hills.

This time as he hit the dirt, Ben rolled sideways, taking another cactus in the side of his lower back. He'd noticed the occasional cactus plant as they'd made their trek through the hills, but hadn't realized how thick the spiny succulents could be under the camouflaging grasses. He hardly felt all the sandburs he'd picked up, what with the long cactus spines that pierced him.

The red dart arced up high while Tyler brought the Cessna back around, slowing down as he approached the hilltop.

Ben looked at his brother through the windshield and shook his head. Stubborn McAlister—Tyler obviously had no intention of leaving him behind. That's what U.S. Air Force training would do to a man.

Against his better judgment, Ben leaped to his feet as the Cessna approached. He'd give it one shot. And if he couldn't hold on, maybe that would convince the headstrong pair on board that they needed to leave Nebraska without him. Ignoring the stabs of pain that shot through him from the cactus spines that dug into his flesh with every movement, Ben positioned himself like a wide receiver ready to make the game-winning catch. He shuffled sideways to nab the landing gear that dangled below the plane like a lure on a fishhook.

Leaping up as the plane passed by just above him, Ben surprised himself by getting both hands solidly around the wheel hub. Half a pull-up later, he'd grabbed the ladder step, and was relieved to discover it had deep grooves on top for added traction. He needed all the help he could get. As he focused on getting his knee up over the fender, he was surprised by the touch of a soft hand on his.

He glanced up, and his heart did a somersault as Ginny smiled down at him.

"Be careful!" He shouted up at her. "Close the door!"

She just grinned in a manner he found entirely unsettling. Between her smile the fact that the plane had begun to pick up speed to stay ahead of the red dart, it was no wonder his stomach was doing flip-flops.

"Give me your hand!" Ginny urged.

Was she crazy? "No! I'll pull you out!"

"I've got my ankles wrapped around the seat base." Her smile didn't falter.

Ben thought of her injured ankle and tried not to cringe. Poor Ginny. He couldn't let her down now. Besides, they'd climbed several hundred feet in the air and a drop from this height would be more than painful.

Even if he managed to avoid landing on another cactus.

Propping one knee on the fender, Ben hoisted himself higher, allowing Ginny to take his hand only once he was fairly certain he was within lunging range of the doorway.

Tyler's excited voice called back to them through the cabin. "Hold on tight, you two!"

That was all the warning they got as the red dart buzzed them so close that, had it not been for Tyler's evasive forty-five-degree tilt, the enemy plane might well have rapped their right wing.

But the downward-tipping angle was more than Ben's foot could handle on the smooth domed hood of the fender. He felt himself slipping off.

Ginny's eyes widened. "Hold on!" she screamed. "Tyler, get this plane righted—now!"

Ben gripped the ladder step with all his might while trying to loosen his hold on Ginny's hand. He might go down, but there was no way he'd allow himself to pull her out after him.

As Tyler steadied the plane, Ben braced himself against the ladder step—the one decent hold he had—then pulled his foot back up to solid contact with the fender. Meanwhile, Ginny's tugging on his other arm had brought his fingers into range of the doorframe.

"Grab the doorway." Ginny heaved backward as his fingertips scraped the frame.

Ben didn't pause to think. He let go of her hand and grabbed the rim of the doorway as instructed while pushing up from the fender. His other foot replaced his hand's grip on the ladder step, and with one more lunge, he had his upper body inside the cabin.

Just in time. Tyler tipped the plane ninety degrees in the other direction, and Ginny rolled back on the floor. Ben scrambled after her, bracing himself against the seat base as he pulled the door shut after him.

The relative silence of the still cabin replaced the roar of the wind.

"Thank God," Ben gasped as soon as he could catch his breath.

"Are you okay?" Ginny asked him.

"I don't know." He winced as the many cactus spines

that pierced him reminded his skin that they hadn't fallen away. "Tyler, how are we doing?"

It took Tyler a couple of seconds to reply. "Dogfight." He whipped the plane into a half turn. "That dude is hot on our tail."

Ginny scrambled toward the front seat. "Can you see the pilot?"

"His helmet covers his face."

Disappointment sagged Ginny's shoulders, but she straightened quickly. "Want me to fly? I do a mean dog-fight."

"This isn't a show." Ben eased himself up beside her in spite of the barbs that tore at him with every movement. "Tyler's a former Air Force pilot. He can handle it." He gripped the seat back in front of him as Tyler spun the plane in a hard turn that threatened to send him reeling.

As he pulled past the red dart, Tyler chided him. "You're the best dogfighter on the plane, big brother. Maybe you'd like to take a turn."

Tempting as the offer might have been, Ben couldn't think straight with the sharp pain that pierced him in so many places he'd lost count. He was pretty sure his lower back wouldn't appreciate sitting in the pilot's seat. "You've got it under control."

"Do I?" A tremor of fear cut through Tyler's voice. "He's got a gun."

SEVEN

Ben pulled Ginny down toward the backseat as the red dart played chicken with his brother in the sky, flying straight at their nose and shooting before pulling aside at the last second and buzzing their wings. He did his best to ignore the floral scent of her hair as it swished past his face. How did the woman manage to smell so good after a daylong trek through the middle of nowhere?

Turning his attention away from Ginny and her alluring fragrance, he asked his brother, "What's he shooting?"

"Some kind of handgun. He held it through the open window."

"How many men are in that plane?"

"I think it's just the pilot." Tyler's voice sounded strained as he pulled the plane wide.

"Any chance we can lose him? We can't risk leading him back to Iowa. He's the last guy I want to know Ginny's whereabouts."

"That's what I'm trying to do, bro. The man knows his stuff."

Ginny didn't take to lying low for long. She put a hand on Ben's shoulder. "What have we got for weapons?" She shouted loud enough for both brothers to hear her over the engine noise.

Tyler chuckled from the pilot's seat. "My cousin Elise uses this plane for her aerial photography business. I can't imagine her packing anything more lethal than a lipstick."

The pretty redhead obviously wasn't about to be dissuaded by his answer. "There's got to be something on this plane we can use," Ginny muttered as she popped open a storage compartment. "Fire extinguisher." She rooted around some more. "Ooh—flares. Those could come in handy."

Ben popped open the other interior storage bay and grinned. "Hold on to the flares for now." He held up his find for her to see. "We've got rope." Then he barked at his brother, "Think you can get on top of him?"

"Do birds fly?" Tyler called back.

"They do until you shoot them." Ginny's words, spoken in a normal voice, were nearly lost among the ambient cabin noise. Though she was holding together courageously, Ben realized the situation had to be difficult for her. And her feet and ankle probably hurt just as bad as his cactus spines.

"Help me get this uncoiled." Ben held out the rope. "Let's get it good and loose. Then we'll drop it slowly onto his propeller as he flies over. If our aim is good, the rope will tangle his prop and bring him down."

"And then what?" Ginny met his eyes.

Her face held a look of trust that penetrated even the growing darkness. Ben struggled to focus on their conversation. "What do you mean?"

"If we bring down the other plane, then what are we going to do? Try to follow him down? Or leave and never know who it was or what happened?"

"I guess that depends." Ben finally uncoiled the long length of the three-quarter-inch-thick nylon rope.

"On what?"

"On whether we're able to bring him down in the first place."

Tyler's words cut through their conversation. "Hey, you two ready back there? I'm almost over him, but it might not be for long."

"Thanks, Tyler." Ben popped the door open a crack, holding it firmly with one hand, and braced his feet against the side of the plane. With the other hand, he started feeding the rope out as Ginny reeled it out to him.

"A little more," he prompted as the tip of the rope bounced in the turbulent air just above the propeller.

Ginny passed forward several more lengths.

"Forward!" Ben called to his brother. "Stay just ahead of him."

He felt the plane ease forward and gave the rope a hearty flick before letting out another fifteen feet of play. The rest of the rope was nearly jerked from his hands. It had caught.

"Stand clear!" Ben shouted as the rope shot past him.

Suddenly Ginny landed against him with a thump. He instinctively body-blocked her from going out the door, his feet bracing against the wall of the plane and his arms tightening around her as though by sheer strength alone he could resist the pull of the plane below them. The frightened look in her eyes sent a jolt of fear straight to his heart. No sooner had Ben followed her gaze to where the rope entangled her shoe then the oversized sneaker pulled free of her foot, snapping out the window and out of view behind them along with the rest of the rope.

Ben slammed the door shut and eased Ginny back onto the rear seat. Bright tears twinkled on her cheeks, reflecting the lights from the instrument panel in the darkness. He hovered over her, unwilling to let go of her after the fear he'd felt at having her nearly ripped from his arms. It had only lasted a fraction of a second, but the terror he'd felt had been so real. And he hadn't even been the one who'd nearly been sucked out of the plane into the chopping blades of the propeller below.

"Ginny?" He pressed his lips near her ear so she could hear him. "Are you okay?"

Her arms trembled as they wrapped around his waist and her body shook with sobs. "That was my sprained foot. I thought it was going to be torn right off my body." Her voice squeaked as she struggled to suck in a breath. "I thought I was a goner."

"No." Ben held her close. "You're okay. You're going to be okay. Thank God, you're going to be okay."

The soothing tone of Ben's voice near her ear helped Ginny catch her breath in spite of the pain. He was right. She was okay. She wasn't convinced God had anything to do with it, but she'd been spared.

Tightening her grip around the strong man who'd saved her, her arm shifted downward on his back.

Ben let out a yelp of pain.

"What's wrong?"

"Cactus spines." He winced.

It took her a moment to sort out what he meant. "You have cactus spines in your back?" She remembered the spines she'd tried to pull from his arm. They'd been stubborn, lined with miniscule barbs that clung to his flesh like microscopic fishhooks, tearing his tissue with every movement.

He nodded. "From when I hit the ground when the plane was buzzing me."

"The plane!" Conflicting thoughts bombarded her. Ginny was concerned about the spines that pierced Ben, but she realized that her attacker was somewhere behind them. "Can we go back and look to see who it was?"

"In this darkness?" Tyler shouted back. "It might take a while. I can radio and tell the authorities to look for him. I checked our coordinates when he went down. They should be able to reach him."

Ginny took a deep breath and absorbed the information.

"Besides," Tyler continued, "after all that monkey business, we've got just enough fuel to make it back to Holyoake. Turning around now won't just waste time—it would waste our whole night."

While Tyler spoke, Ben eased himself onto the bench seat beside her. She scooted back to give him room and watched as he winced when his back brushed the seat.

"Head for Holyoake, then." Ginny raised her voice so Tyler could hear her. "And can you turn the cabin lights on, please?"

"Sure thing."

The sudden burst of illumination startled her eyes, but she quickly focused on Ben's injury, sucking in a sharp breath when she saw the torn and bloodied fabric of his shirt that was stabbed through with cactus spines.

"Is there a first aid kit onboard?" she asked loudly.

"I saw one in the storage compartment where I found the rope."

"Good." Ginny unclasped the latch on the compartment. "What about needle-nose pliers?"

A small tool kit supplied the pliers, as well as scissors to cut away the tattered section of Ben's shirt so she could see to remove the barbs. She knew it had to hurt every time she pulled one out, but Ben didn't make a sound.

"I'm sorry," she apologized for the fifteenth time as she applied antiseptic to the wounds, blowing gently on each spot in an attempt to minimize the stinging. His well-muscled back was furiously inflamed. She felt horrible about all he'd endured.

"While you're working on that," Tyler called from the front seat, "Elise packed you a snack." He tossed back a small soft-sided cooler.

Ginny caught the bundle with a cry of joy and hastily unzipped it.

"What's in it?" Ben asked.

"I don't care if it's bread and water—" She squealed happily when she saw the contents. "Chocolate!" She quickly unwrapped one of the foil-wrapped candies and, though she was tempted to gulp it down in one bite, she handed it to Ben. "Eat up, there's plenty."

"Thanks." He popped it into his mouth with a satisfied groan.

"Thank Elise. She has excellent taste." Ginny grinned and unwrapped a chocolate for herself, then uncapped a couple of cold sodas. "Oh, thank God." She sighed after taking a long draught.

It wasn't until she heard the words on her lips that she wondered where they'd come from. She hadn't thanked God since before her father's death. Did she really think God had provided the chocolate, Tyler and the plane that rescued them? Surely she'd only spoken the phrase simply because she'd heard Ben talk about God so many times that day. She'd long ago given up on God's protection. And yet, how had Tyler found them?

Getting back to work plucking cactus spines from Ben's knee, Ginny asked Tyler, "How did you know to come looking for us?"

Their pilot chuckled from the front seat. "Ben called this morning to let us know you were headed home. Elise was hoping you'd be there by lunchtime. When you didn't show, she started getting worried. Then when you couldn't be reached on your cell phones, she started threatening to come get you herself. Of course, Cutch wouldn't let her do that."

"Cutch wouldn't let her fly her own plane?" Ginny cringed at the thought. Surely her brother wasn't that kind of guy, was he?

"Nope."

"Why not?"

The McAlister men both chuckled. "You'll have to ask your brother about that one." Ben sounded amused.

Ginny felt her head go hot at the thought of her brother limiting his new wife's freedoms. But then, what did she expect? Hadn't Kevin tried to do the same to her? That was such a large part of why their relationship hadn't worked out. And her roommate Megan's marriage had failed when her husband had tried to micromanage her activities. Ginny was going to give her big brother a piece of her mind when she got the chance.

And meanwhile, the way Ben chuckled with pleasure at the whole scenario caused Ginny to check her growing feelings for him. So Ben thought it was amusing when a man controlled a woman, did he? She felt grateful for all he'd done to rescue her that day, and for the selfless way he'd carried her through the desert. And her heart swelled with compassion as she pulled the prickly cactus barbs from his angry flesh. But that didn't mean she had feelings for him. She couldn't possibly. She wasn't the kind of woman who would ever let a man control her.

The deep darkness of night shrouded the countryside when they finally touched down at the McAlister airfield in rural Holyoake County, and even the crickets had gone to sleep. Ben helped Ginny disembark. Between her lone oversized shoe and her turned ankle, she was a little unsteady on her feet.

But still the stubborn beauty insisted on standing on her own. Ben wondered at her independence. She'd been quiet for most of the flight home. Though he'd attributed her silence to exhaustion and the noise of the small plane that discouraged conversation, now he wondered at the way she pushed away from him and deliberately put space between them. Was she that eager to get away from him?

Elise and Cutch had hurried out of the airfield office as the plane touched down, followed by Ginny's mother, Anita McCutcheon, and Ben's uncle, Bill McAlister, who was Elise's father. Cutch grabbed his little sister in a quick hug. "Welcome home, Ginny."

Cutch had barely spoken when Ginny's mother reached her. Anita quickly had her daughter enfolded in her ample embrace.

"Oh, Ginny!" Anita shrieked as she patted her daughter's cheeks and smoothed her hair, in her motherly way seeming to reassure herself that her daughter really was safely home. "Ginny, you had us so worried! What happened? What took you so long? I thought you were flying your own plane? We were expecting you in time for a late lunch, and I was so worried. I said to Bill, 'Honey, where is that daughter of mine?'"

Ginny's head snapped back from her mother's smothering. "Bill? Honey?" Confusion warred on her face.

Ben cringed inwardly. He'd hoped Ginny's mom would have revealed her new relationship a little more delicately, but obviously in her distressed condition, she hadn't thought about what she was saying.

He watched Anita's face turn white as she realized what she'd said. Anita's husband, Ginny's father, had died over three months before, after a nine-year battle with cancer.

But Ben's uncle Bill had been engaged to Anita when they were young, before she'd married Cutch and Ginny's father. Their new relationship had seemingly sprung up right where the old one left off. Though it seemed like a natural fit to those who were around them regularly, Ben knew the news had to be jarring to Ginny, who was still mourning the loss of her father.

Bill McAlister stepped forward and placed his hand on Anita's shoulder. "Ginny, your mother and I have been seeing each other—" he began.

But Ginny had obviously had enough for one day. She backed away, hobbling on her bad ankle. "No." She shook her head. "You can't."

Ben couldn't stand watching the pain rise to her face.

"I need to go." She turned her back to them.

Anita and Bill gave each other sympathetic looks, as though both of them looked to the other for guidance on how to respond. Elise and Cutch looked at each other with the same questioning concern.

"Should I go after her?" Anita whispered to Bill.

"I think she needs some space right now," he advised quietly. As Elise's father, Bill knew a thing or two about parenting a strong-willed young woman.

Unable to stand the sight of Ginny hobbling away looking so alone, Ben fell into step beside her. "Need a lift?" His car was still parked where he'd left it at the airfield office the day before when he'd set out for Wyoming.

Ginny looked up at him and sniffled. "Yes." She took a couple more steps and winced. "Can I lean on you?"

His arm flew around her, supporting her injured side. "Sure thing."

"Thanks. Just get me out of here. I can't talk to her. I can't think about…that."

Ginny's whole body shuddered at what Ben knew had to

be highly unwelcome news. If he'd had any idea that Anita would let the cat out of the bag so suddenly, Ben would have given Ginny more warning ahead of time. As it was, he'd assumed it was Anita and Bill's story to tell, and he'd respected their relationship to each other and to Ginny. But the tumultuous events of the day had obviously been too much for everyone.

"Where are we headed?" he asked once Ginny had settled into the passenger seat and he'd gotten his Ford Mustang in gear.

"I don't care. Just get me away from here. I usually stay at my mom's when I'm home, but—" she made another face. "How serious are they, Ben? She called him 'honey.'"

Unsure where to start, Ben cleared his throat as he pulled out onto the gravel road. "You know they were engaged years ago, before your mom and dad were married."

"Cutch mentioned that to me a while back. I thought it was strange."

"Apparently that's what started the feud in earnest— your father stole my Uncle Bill's fiancée while Bill was overseas serving his country. He got home thinking Anita was going to marry him, and there she was married to your dad and pregnant with your brother."

Ginny's hand covered her mouth. "Cutch didn't mention that part."

"He probably thought it was your mother's place to explain it all." Ben shook his head regretfully as he turned the corner to the blacktop road that led into town. "I thought so, too, or I'd have given you more warning."

His words were cut short by the sound of music.

"Your phone." Ginny startled and looked at Ben's phone which he'd tossed in the center console. "It's Megan. I wonder why she's calling at this hour." Ginny had given Megan Ben's number, since her own phone had been destroyed in the fire. She looked to Ben for permission, then answered his phone.

Between the quiet in the car and the high volume of Megan's frantic voice, Ben couldn't avoid hearing both sides of the conversation.

"Ginger! Where have you been? Why didn't you answer your phone?"

"It's a long story. What's wrong?"

"Remember Bobby Burbank?"

Ginny made a face into the phone. "The guy who attacked me in the hangar yesterday? What about him?"

"They don't know where he is. He escaped from jail!"

EIGHT

Ginny quizzed Megan on everything she knew about Bobby Burbank's jail break and his possible whereabouts. Unfortunately, neither Megan nor the authorities seemed to know much about where he'd gone, or even how or when he'd escaped. They'd checked on him several times and assumed he was sleeping under a billowed blanket in his cell. When they'd tried to rouse him for lunch, they'd found nothing but air.

"How could that happen?" Ginny wondered aloud, thinking back to Jim and Roger, the deputies who'd questioned her after the attack the day before. She had sensed a certain level of resentment on their part toward the Dare Divas and the trouble they'd brought to Wyoming. But had their resentment caused their negligence? Or had they been complicit in Bobby's escape?

Fear raised the pitch of Megan's voice. "I don't feel safe here, Ginger. I'm worried about Noah and everything that's going on, what with the trailer burning down and everything."

"Is there anywhere you can go? Home?" Her instinct was to invite Megan to bring her young son to Holyoake, but Ben had insisted on telling no one where they'd gone. But surely it wouldn't hurt to invite her dear friend? Ginny would never forgive herself if anything happened to Megan or Noah, especially if there had been something she could have done to help.

"I don't know where to go." Megan sounded like she was fighting back frightened tears. "If I go home to Alabama, my ex-husband will find me. He's already tried to take Noah before. I don't have anyone else except the Dare Divas, and I just don't feel safe here with that man on the loose."

As Ben pulled the Mustang to a stop near the Holyoake Riverside Park, Ginny closed her eyes, wishing she could pray for guidance like Ben seemed to do so easily. But why would the God who took her father away pay any attention to her prayers now?

"Megan, do you still have the key I gave you to the plane Ben flew up in yesterday?" Ginny had given her friend the key in case Ben's plane needed to be moved from where they'd parked it.

"Of course. You made me promise not to lose it."

"Do you want to fly it out to come visit me?"

"Ginger!" Megan gasped happily. "I'd love to, but I don't know where you are. You refused to tell anyone."

"I know. And you can't tell anyone else." Ginny turned her head away as a scowling Ben leaned across the seat in her face.

"No, Ginny," he whispered, "don't tell *anyone* where you are."

But Ginny wasn't about to let a man control her. Maybe Cutch could keep Elise from flying, and maybe Bill McAlister had won over her mom in spite of her recent loss, but Ben's interference only made Ginny that much more determined to tell Megan where she was staying. Megan was her friend, and Ginny trusted her. She'd known her a lot longer than she'd known Ben.

Rattling off instructions for how to find both Holyoake and the McCutcheon farmstead, Ginny found she had to lean away from Ben and even cover the phone before he finally gave up trying to stop her and crossed his arms over his chest, sulking in the driver's seat.

Ginny gave him a satisfied smile as she closed the phone. Everything else in her world might be crazy, but she still had control over her own decisions. She could still help out a friend.

To her surprise, Ben didn't say anything, though the corner of his eye twitched as she watched him, waiting for an outburst or any sort of response. She could feel the frustration radiating off him.

"I know you don't think Megan can be trusted," Ginny began slowly, already feeling a twinge of guilt after all Ben had done to help her, and feeling the need to justify her decision.

"It doesn't matter what I think, does it?" Ben turned to her with eyes that looked sad instead of angry in the light from the streetlamps that illuminated the park. He sighed. "I just hope you're right, Ginny. I hope, for your sake, that Megan really isn't involved in any of this. And I really hope no one was listening in on that conversation."

Resenting the guilt she felt at Ben's response, she settled back into her seat. "You can take me to my mom's house now. I'd rather deal with her right now than with you."

Ben drove in silence, his tired mind slogging through the unfamiliar onslaught of emotions he felt. Ginny was obviously upset with him, but he had no clue how to talk any sense into her.

It seemed illogical, after all the terrifying situations he'd faced in his career in the Air Force, that the little red-headed girl from down the road could terrify him so much.

But he cared deeply about Ginny's opinion of him and he didn't want to do anything to upset her further.

As his car drew closer to the McCutcheon farmstead, Ben tried to break down the situation in his head. He didn't know how to talk to Ginny, but he needed to say something. She seemed to be ignoring the facts that Bobby Burbank was on the loose, and that they still didn't know what had happened to the pilot of the plane they'd dropped rope on over the sand hills. They didn't even know who or how many people were after Ginny. Her life was still in danger. He couldn't let the fact that she was upset with him keep him from trying to protect her.

She might hate him forever, but Ben figured it didn't matter. After Cutch and Elise's wedding celebration, Ginny was going to fly back to Wyoming and he'd likely never see her again anyway. So she could get as mad at him as she wanted and it still wouldn't matter. At least she'd be alive to hate him.

He pulled the Mustang to a stop in the next driveway.

Ginny glared at him. "This is the McAlister place. What are we doing here?"

"It's my Uncle Bill's house. The house where Elise grew up, but she and Cutch have a place in town now. Doesn't look like Bill is home yet."

"I don't want to talk to Bill."

"I didn't stop here for you to talk to Bill. I stopped so you would talk to me."

"I don't want—"

Ben didn't give her a chance to finish her protest. "Bobby Burbank broke out of jail," he reminded her sharply. "Are you forgetting that? He tracked you from New Jersey to Wyoming, and he could track you down again."

"Yeah, and if he looks in the phone book for McAlister,

he'll probably end up *here*." Ginny gestured to the McAlister house. "Now can you take me to my mother's house so I can rest?"

"We don't know yet who was piloting the Dare Divas plane that attacked us over Nebraska."

Ginny rubbed her eyes with her fingertips. "Maybe it was Bobby Burbank."

"He stole a Dare Divas plane?" Ben shook his head. "If he was behind this, I can't imagine that he was working alone. He would have had to have access to your plane this morning. And Kristy Keller's plane three months ago. Besides, the deputies already determined that Bobby Burbank was at work when those shots were fired at you."

For a moment Ginny simply made a thoughtful face and worried her lower lip. Then she offered, "I'll call Doug Adolph tomorrow morning and find out if there's anything to connect Bobby Burbank to Kristy Keller's accident. And maybe Zeke Ward knows something about the mechanics involved. He's the one who reported the other suspicious mechanical problems before they caused an accident."

Relieved that she was taking the situation seriously, Ben started the engine again and turned the car around, heading back up the road to the McCutcheon place. "Don't forget your security guy. In fact, I want to talk to Earl myself and get the names of everyone who's worked security under him in the last six months, both in New Jersey and in Wyoming. It seems to me there's been a breach of protection."

Ginny nodded. "Okay. But can we do all that tomorrow? I'm exhausted and all those people I need to talk to are probably asleep right now anyway."

"Tomorrow." Ben agreed. "I'm going to check on everyone who's had access to you and the Dare Divas planes. And I want you to tell me about anything you can think of that could in any way be related to this mess, no matter how insignificant it may seem, as well as everything you can remember about Kristy Keller's accident."

"I don't like talking about Kristy's accident," Ginny warned him in a whisper.

"I'm sorry to make you discuss it. I'm sorry any of this mess has happened to you." He slowed the car as they approached the driveway. "But I don't know of any other way to make it stop."

Ginny pinched her eyes shut for a silent moment before unbuckling her seat belt as the car came to a stop. "Okay."

"Need a hand getting to the front door?" Ben knew her ankle had to be throbbing.

She nodded, and Ben jumped out and trotted around to open the passenger door for her. He propped up her injured side as he had already so many times that night. Her lean arm felt familiar as it encircled his shoulder, and her trim waist tucked perfectly under his supporting hand.

"I'm sorry to be such a burden," Ginny apologized as she made her way wearily toward the front steps.

"You're not a burden. I'm just glad I can help."

Ginny hopped on her good foot up the steps, leaning heavily on Ben's shoulder. When she reached the top, she smiled up at him. It wasn't one of her trademark poster-pretty smiles, but a sincere, if weary, smile of gratitude that Ben found more alluring still. For an instant he felt the impulse to kiss her good-night right there under the stars.

But who was he fooling? She was Ginger McAlister, the Dare Divas' frontwoman. She was way out of his league, and only a few minutes before she'd been plenty upset with him.

Besides, he knew from everything she'd said that she loved flying and had no intention of giving up the stunt circuit any time soon. Whereas Ben had come home to Holyoake to settle down and help run the family airfield. Ginny belonged in New Jersey. Ben belonged in Iowa. Those two places were pretty far apart.

Ben helped Ginny to the front door, and she propped it open, transferring her weight to the doorframe as she leaned against the sturdy structure for support.

"I'm sorry I snapped at you earlier." Ginny looked up at him repentantly. "I just couldn't *not* help Megan."

"Megan's lucky to have a friend like you."

Ginny's smile rose closer to her eyes, which twinkled softly in the starlight. "I'm lucky to have a friend like you," she whispered.

The urge to kiss her was so overwhelming, Ben quickly turned away. "Good night," he called back as he nearly ran down the steps. "Get some sleep." He dived into his car, feeling like a coward who'd turned tail and run at the first hint of danger.

But as he watched Ginny hop inside and close the door behind her, he realized he *was* in danger—and not just from whoever was out to kill Ginny. He was in danger of falling in love with her. And he had absolutely no business doing that.

Ginny awoke late the next morning, groggy from pain. Her leg felt heavy as she lifted the swollen mass that had been her ankle. Eww. Black-and-blue puffiness extended all the way to her toes. She just hoped the swelling would go down in time for her to wear her bridesmaid sandals for Cutch and Elise's wedding celebration.

After showering on one foot, Ginny hopped back down the hall to her old bedroom. She rooted around in a dresser full of the clothes she'd left behind when she'd run off to become a stunt pilot at age eighteen. Her tastes may have

Send For
2 FREE BOOKS
Today!

I accept your offer!

Please send me two free
Love Inspired® Suspense
novels and two mystery
gifts (gifts worth about $10).
I understand that these books
are completely free—even
the shipping and handling will
be paid—and I am under no
obligation to purchase anything, ever,
as explained on the back of this card.

❏ I prefer the regular-print edition
123/323 IDL FEMM

❏ I prefer the larger-print edition
110/310 IDL FEMM

Please Print

FIRST NAME

LAST NAME

ADDRESS

APT.#	CITY

STATE/PROV.	ZIP/POSTAL CODE

**Visit us online at
www.ReaderService.com**

NO POSTAGE
NECESSARY
IF MAILED
IN THE
UNITED STATES

BUSINESS REPLY MAIL
FIRST-CLASS MAIL   PERMIT NO. 717   BUFFALO, NY

POSTAGE WILL BE PAID BY ADDRESSEE

THE READER SERVICE
PO BOX 1867
BUFFALO NY 14240-9952

matured a bit in the eight years since, and the things she'd left behind had never been her favorites or she wouldn't have left them, but at least they still fit. All except the socks, which refused to go past the toes of her injured foot.

Making a face at her obstinate appendage, she shoved Veronica's lone remaining sneaker onto her good foot and left the other one bare before hobbling down the hall and downstairs.

Her mother looked up from the morning paper and smiled, though her eyes were shadowed with a wary look. Ginny had arrived home before her mother the night before, and had gone straight to bed. She hadn't seen her since their brief embrace at the airport.

"Can I get you some breakfast? I made those cinnamon rolls you always liked."

"Awesome." Ginny lowered herself into a chair and shuffled around until she got her injured leg propped up on a nearby seat.

"Do you want an ice pack for that?" Anita McCutcheon asked as she headed toward a foil-covered pan.

"I don't know if I should ice it or use a heat pack."

"Bill hurt his knee a couple of months ago and the doctor said—"

Tension gripped Ginny at the mention of her mother's new beau. "You were seeing Bill a couple of *months* ago?" Ginny had hoped at the very least that her mother had only recently started dating Bill.

Red color flooded her mother's pale face. "I brought him dinner when he got hurt. That was kind of how we started seeing each other. Well, that and all the plans for Cutch and Elise's wedding." Anita scooped a large, gooey caramel roll onto a plate. "Do you want this warm?"

Unsure how she could eat with her mother talking about

Bill, Ginny shrugged. "I don't care." She bit back the bitter questions she wanted to pose about whether her father's body had even been cold in the ground before Anita had taken up with Bill. Anger wouldn't help. In her head, she knew that. But between the pain radiating up her leg and the sense of betrayal she felt on behalf of her father's memory, Ginny had a difficult time keeping her mouth shut.

Her mother settled the plate onto the table in front of her. "Can I get you anything else? Something to drink? We've got milk, orange juice or coffee."

Awkwardness saturated her words.

"Milk would be great." Ginny reached for the roll. "And if you have any painkillers in this house, I could use the maximum dosage."

Silently Anita McCutcheon served up a glass of milk with a side of painkillers before sitting down in the chair opposite Ginny. "I'm sorry for the way you found out about me and Bill." She gripped her coffee with rigid hands.

Ginny could tell her mother felt bad. She could tell she was trying to make things right. But every time Ginny thought about the way her mother and Bill had acted like a cozy couple, her stomach turned. Even the delicious caramel roll felt like plaster in her mouth, and she struggled to swallow. Unable to protest through the sticky mouthful of roll, she sat, hobbled by her ankle, and endured the explanation she didn't want to hear.

"The doctors said your father was going to die nine years ago, Ginny," Anita explained. "I came to terms with that. I didn't like it, we vowed to fight it, but I accepted the likelihood that he wouldn't be around—that we'd never retire and enjoy grandchildren together like we'd always planned."

Ginny felt her throat tighten. She was never going to get a single bite down at this rate.

"His cancer came back three times," Anita continued. "He fought hard. I was so proud of him. I loved him to the very end. I love him still. But he's not here any longer, and I'm just so tired of grieving. I grieved for nine years, Ginny, and took care of him all that time, by his side day and night." She looked at her daughter imploringly. "I just want to live again."

Tears dripped down Ginny's cheeks and she finally gave up trying to swallow and placed the bite of caramel roll in a napkin. She missed her father—missed that he'd never get to hold her children on his lap or take them fishing like her own grandfather had taken her and Cutch when they were little. Being home only made the buried pain that much worse.

After an awkward silence, Anita leaned back and reflected, "Not everyone finds love in this world. Finding it once is a blessing. Finding it twice is a miracle." She smiled broadly. "Bill and I feel grateful to have found one another again. I hope some day you can be happy for us."

Ginny stared at her napkin. Her mother's words rocked around in her mind, reminding her of her ill-fated relationship with Kevin. He'd wanted her to give up flying, to settle down and be a stay-at-home kind of wife. Had they really been in love? He was married now, with kids, somewhere in Vermont. At least he'd found love. Twice? No. Looking back, Ginny thought she and Kevin must not have really been in love. How could she have been in love with someone who tried to limit her freedom?

The ringing phone cut through her thoughts. Anita hopped up to answer it, her voice cheerful as she informed the caller, "She's finally up!" before passing the phone to

Ginny. "It's Ben," she explained out loud, then mouthed, "he's been calling all morning."

Ginny swallowed back the stubborn lump in her throat and took the phone, grateful to have an excuse to end the conversation with her mother, and maybe just a little bit excited to hear Ben's voice. "Can you come pick me up?" she asked eagerly.

When Ben agreed, Ginny felt a trepidatious mixture of relief and dread. Ben had promised to help her catch whoever had been causing her so much trouble lately. Ginny felt hopeful that the authorities might have found the wreck of the red plane that had attacked them the night before. Maybe they'd catch this would-be killer after all. Ginny couldn't wait to have her freedom back.

But at the same time, the road before her seemed cloaked in foreboding danger. How many more close calls would she have to endure before her attacker was caught? Perhaps worst of all, there was a part of her that wasn't looking forward to learning her attacker's identity. Did one of the people she worked with and trusted secretly want her dead?

Ben pulled up at the McCutcheon house and tried to talk down his heart, which was jumping around in his chest at the thought of seeing Ginny again. He was just glad she wasn't still upset with him—that was all. And he was glad no one had tried to harm her since he'd seen her last.

Leaping up the front porch steps in a single bound, he stopped close beside her as she hopped through the front door, her swollen foot hovering uselessly a few inches above the floor.

"Need a hand?"

When she reached for him automatically and leaned against his shoulder as they navigated their way down the steps, Ben attributed his soaring heart to the fact that she trusted him. And he was happy to be of some help to her.

He tried to wipe the silly grin off his face. After all, they had serious issues to discuss. "Where would you like to go first?"

"The car dealership in town," Ginny answered without hesitation.

Her request took him off guard. "Why there?"

"They rent cars. I need something to drive myself around. I can't depend upon other people the whole time I'm here."

Ben balked at the idea of Ginny driving around alone. She was still so vulnerable. And how could he shield her from danger if she had her own car? "Can you drive with your injured ankle?"

"I'll rent an automatic." She leaned against the passenger side of his Mustang and looked up at him. "It only takes one good foot."

"Do you really need a car? I can drive you anywhere you need to go."

A frustrated look crossed Ginny's face, and Ben realized she looked as though she'd had an emotional morning all ready. "I need my freedom."

"Even when there's someone after you?"

Ginny crossed her arms and glared at him. "This is *exactly* the reason why I need a car. I shouldn't have to justify my reasons every time I want to go somewhere."

Ben realized he must have hit a nerve. But he appreciated the fact that she wanted her freedom. He knew he wouldn't like having to depend on someone else so much. "To the dealership it is, then." He helped her into her seat before trotting around to the driver's side.

As he put the car in gear, he caught Ginny up on what had happened since they'd last been together. "Your friend

Megan radioed the airfield just as I was leaving. She should be landing in Holyoake shortly."

"Excellent!" Ginny grinned. "I'll go see her as soon as I rent a car."

"Tyler mentioned bringing Megan and Noah into town for lunch. I thought maybe we could meet up with them at Nana's Café. You still need that cheeseburger you were talking about yesterday."

Ginny assessed the invitation aloud. "Cutch and Elise invited me over to their place for supper, but I don't have anywhere I need to be until then. And I really should catch up with Megan after all she's been through." She nodded as she agreed to the idea. "Sounds like a plan."

It sounded more like a double date to Ben, but he wasn't about to mention that to Ginny.

To Ben's relief, renting a car didn't take long at the small-town dealership, and Ginny finished signing the paperwork while Ben called his brother to solidify their lunch plans.

"Megan and Noah landed. Tyler's bringing them to join us at Nana's Café." He held her car door open as Ginny eased her injured leg into the rental car.

"Perfect. If it eases your concern about my ability to drive, you can follow me over there," she offered, smiling up at him.

Ben agreed, and after an uneventful drive, they pulled to a stop in the busy parking lot of Nana's Café just in time to see Tyler carrying Noah toward the entrance with Megan at his side. The sight of his little brother acting like a family man almost made Ben do a double take. Tyler didn't look nearly as awkward as Ben might have thought. Megan approached Ginny with arms wide open, squeezing her in a grateful hug before following Tyler inside the homey eating establishment.

"Thank you so much for letting me hide out here, Ginger." Megan gushed as they entered the cozy café. "Your cousin has been very helpful." Megan watched as Tyler led Noah to the kids' activity table the small-town café provided.

"Uh, actually—" Ginny's face colored to match her hair "—he's not really my cousin. I mean, my brother is married to Ben and Tyler's cousin Elise…" She faltered through her words awkwardly.

"But you're all McAlisters." Megan looked puzzled.

Ben recalled that Ginny had gone solely by the name of Ginger McAlister on the flying circuit. Megan was likely unaware of Ginny's real name—and for her safety, he didn't want anyone else to learn who she really was.

Steering the adults to a booth near the activity table where Noah played, Ben encouraged them to sit plenty close enough for Megan to keep an eye on her son. "Ginger McAlister is Ginny's flying name. She's not really a McAlister."

"Oh!" Megan's eyes widened. "Ginny?" The name sounded unfamiliar as she spoke it. "Why did you choose to fly under the McAlister name?"

As Ginny's face went red, Ben repeated the question as Tyler joined them at the booth. "Yes, Ginny, why did you choose to fly under the McAlister name?"

Ginny looked as though she wanted to disappear into the back of the booth, where the ladies sat opposite the McAlister men. "I didn't want to fly under my own name. Doug and Ron encouraged all of us to change our names in the beginning." Ginny accepted a menu from the waitress with thanks and buried her face in the pages.

Ben cleared his throat and she peeked her blue eyes over the rim at him.

"I thought you were having the cheeseburger?" He'd

been curious to hear Ginny's real reasons for choosing the
McAlister name ever since he'd realized the true identity
of the redheaded aviatrix, and he didn't believe for one
second that her "running off to join the circus" excuse was
all there was to it.

"So, why *did* you choose to fly as a McAlister?" he
asked again as soon as the waitress disappeared.

Setting down her menu with a resolute expression,
Ginny explained, "I figured I'd need a name I could answer
to—something my ears would prick up at, so I wouldn't
snub my fans by walking right past them when they called
a name I wasn't used to. Ginger sounds a lot like Ginny."

"And McAlister?" Ben could tell Ginny was trying to
make it sound as though the question was a trivial one, but
the furious blush on her cheeks told him otherwise. He'd
tapped into an emotion that ran deep. But why?

Ginny rolled her eyes. "That silly feud, for one thing.
I never heard the name McAlister without my ears prick-
ing up. We were supposed to avoid you folks, you know,
but your names were in the news all the time, first with all
your high school sports accomplishments, then when you
joined the Air Force and every time you'd come home to
march in a parade or talk to kids at the school. Besides,
McAlister sounds a little like McCutcheon. I figured it was
a name I could answer to. That's why I chose it."

Her answer was different enough from what she'd told
him in the field two days before that Ben wanted to press
further, but Tyler had been looking like he wanted to talk
ever since he'd joined them at the booth. Now he leaned
across the booth. "I got a call on my way into town from
those investigators that looked into that red plane that came
after us last night."

Ben had been eagerly waiting for news on the plane's
status. "What were they able to tell you?" He knew his

savvy private investigator brother would have known just the things to say to get as much information as possible from the authorities.

"It had crashed. There wasn't much left of it, but they did find a body."

"Were they able to make a positive ID?"

"It's not official, but it looks like the same guy that broke out of jail, the one who attacked Ginny. Bobby Burbank?"

Ginny gasped. "He was behind everything, then." Remorse filled her words. "I hate to think that we killed him."

"But Ging—er, Ginny." Megan adjusted to Ginny's hometown name. "This guy attacked you. Maybe now this will all be over."

"Not so fast." Tyler cautioned. "Bobby Burbank's body was found bound hand and foot. They're speculating he was dead before the plane ever hit the ground."

NINE

"No!" Ginny's wail startled the waitress who'd returned to take their orders. Ben reached across the table and squeezed her hand. With his comforting grip keeping her just on the sane side of panic, Ginny managed to place her order before her roiling insides overflowed.

"Someone else was flying that plane? Bobby wasn't working alone?" Ginny's questions poured out in a rushed whisper once the waitress departed with their orders.

Tyler looked apologetic. "They don't know much of anything for sure yet. One door of the plane was wide open. Whether it was knocked open on impact or left open by the pilot bailing out, we don't know. But they did say it seemed highly unlikely that Bobby could have been the person piloting the plane, bound like he was, and likely dead already. They'll have to do some more tests and make a definite ID before they can say anything for sure, but that's what we know now."

"Thank you for getting those answers," Ginny said, though what she wanted to do was scream in frustration. She looked at Ben. "I thought you said stalkers usually worked alone?"

"They do." Ben looked just as frustrated as she felt. "Perhaps whoever made the previous attempts on your life hired Bobby in order to make it look like a stalker attack. Then when his attempt failed, they killed him to keep him quiet."

Megan had been listening with a horrified expression, and now shook her head. "So many planes took off yesterday. I had no idea one of them might be flown by your attacker. I'm so glad I got Noah out of there. At least we'll be safer now that this Bobby fellow is dead."

Much as Ginny wanted to offer comforting words to her friend, she didn't think Megan's assessment was true. "If the person who hired Bobby is still at large…" she began, but was unsure how to finish her statement without further frightening Megan.

Ben still had hold of her hand across the table, and now he gave it a comforting squeeze. "We'll find him. Tyler has six years' experience as a private investigator. If there's a trail to find, he'll find it." He looked back and forth between Ginny and Megan. "Can you ladies tell us everything you can recall about the previous incidents? No detail is too small to be unimportant."

With Megan's help, Ginny was able to relay the unusual mechanical problems that Zeke Ward and his fellow mechanics had reported over the previous weeks—suspicious incidents where plane engines had apparently been tampered with, likely in hopes of bringing the plane and its pilot down in a fiery crash.

"How does that compare to the mechanical analysis of Kristy Keller's engine following her crash?" Ben asked after Ginny had recalled all she could of the other incidents.

A guilty knot formed in Ginny's stomach, and a familiar pain shot through her heart. "It wasn't really *Kristy's* engine. Kristy was flying my plane. I was on my way back from my father's funeral, but I was running late. Kristy flew my opening segment for me."

Ben's eyes narrowed. "You would have been at the controls?"

Pain tore through Ginny. She couldn't stand it. "Excuse me." She apologized and headed for the front door, ignoring the throbbing ache in her ankle as she limped past the booths and tables.

"Ginny!" Ben caught up to her in the parking lot as she hobbled toward her rental car.

She couldn't hide the tears she felt slipping from her eyes. "You'll have to eat my cheeseburger for me, Ben."

He didn't acknowledge her statement, but pulled her into his strong arms.

For a second Ginny considered pushing him away, but her heart hurt, and being in Ben's arms was the only thing that had helped to ease that pain before. She buried her face against his shoulder and squeezed out a silent sob. "It should have been me," she gasped when she could finally speak. "I should have been injured, not Kristy."

"No." Ben's bass voice rumbled through his chest. "No one should have gotten hurt. None of you girls deserved that accident. Whoever's after you—" His arms tightened around her as his words dropped away.

After a few moments his grip eased and Ginny reluctantly pulled her head back so she could look up at him.

"We'll find whoever's after you," Ben promised. "I'll keep you safe."

The intensity in his expression eased the torment of her heart. What was it about this man that made her hope that things might really turn out all right after all?

Much as she wanted to bury her face in his shoulder again, Ginny knew Tyler and Megan had to be wondering what had happened to them. "We can talk more after lunch," she offered.

"Good." Ben smiled. "Because I still haven't heard any details on those gunshots."

They suspended any worrisome talk as Noah joined them at the booth to eat. After enjoying a delicious meal, Ben picked up the tab and helped Ginny out to the parking lot. Megan insisted on getting a hotel room in spite of Ginny's invitation that she stay at the McCutcheon home. Tyler had begun background checks on all the names Ben had given him, and was hoping to have information waiting for him at the airfield office across town. Though Tyler had offered to drop Megan off at her hotel, Ben wanted answers sooner than that.

"Megan can drive my car. I'll ride with Ginny. We need to talk anyway," Ben insisted, and was glad when no one argued.

If anything, Megan looked eagerly at Ben's Mustang as he handed over the keys and helped her get Noah's car seat buckled in.

Then he climbed into the passenger side of Ginny's rental car.

"I can't believe you let Megan borrow your Mustang." Ginny started the rental car.

"She flew my plane without incident," Ben reminded her. "Besides, your rental agreement says you're the only one who can drive this car. And Tyler needs to focus on the investigation assignment I gave him. You saw how much Megan distracted him."

Ginny giggled. "You'd think he'd never seen a pretty pilot before."

"Not one he wasn't already related to." Ben redirected the conversation in the direction he wanted it to go. "What can you tell me about these gunshots that narrowly missed hitting you a few weeks ago?"

Ginny launched into a detailed recounting of both incidents, and Ben was disappointed by how very little there was to either story.

"I thought it was an insect buzzing by my ear, until I heard the bullets hit the building. Then I ducked and ran. There wasn't time to think. The second time I didn't hear anything, so the shots must not have come quite as close. I saw the bullets hit the building, saw the holes and ran. I don't know how I missed getting hit."

"God was watching out for you," Ben concluded.

Ginny's derisive snort surprised Ben.

"Don't you think God was protecting you?" he asked.

"Sure." She rolled her eyes and turned the car down the hilly gravel road that led to the McCutcheon place nestled on the edge of the loess hills of southwestern Iowa. "Just like God protected my dad from cancer? Just like God protected Kristy?"

"I thought Kristy was going to be okay?" Ben was taken aback by Ginny's sarcasm.

"She broke both her legs." Ginny accelerated with her one good foot. "She had burns over twenty percent of her body. She could have *died*."

"But she didn't." Ben wasn't sure where Ginny was coming from with her angry words toward God. He understood how upsetting her father's death had been, but he hadn't realized how much it had shaken her faith. He wished he knew what to say to comfort her.

They topped a hill, and the tiny rental car bounced in the air.

Ginny gasped.

Ben looked at her with concern, wondering if the bounce

had reminded her of the turbulence they'd experienced while flying just before the plane's engine had cut out.

But Ginny had a good reason for looking terrified. All the lights on the dashboard glowed ominously. The engine had died.

"Ben!" Ginny screamed, looking to him imploringly. The car careened down the steep hill. "I can't steer. The power steering went out with the engine!"

"Brake! Can you brake?"

While Ginny shuffled her injured foot so she could reach the brake pedal, Ben reached over and tried to muscle the steering wheel into a straight line. The steep road was rimmed on either side by deep ditches bordered with trees. Nothing they wanted to drive into, not if they wanted to survive.

The tiny rental car began to fishtail crazily.

"Don't stomp on it!" Ben reminded her. "Not on this gravel. Pump the brake gently. Gently. There you go. You're going to be okay. Stay calm. We're slowing down."

And indeed, they were. Ginny brought the car to rest part way up the next hill. Ben had managed to muscle the stiff steering wheel to the right, just enough to get them out of the middle of the road and the path of anything that might come up over the top of the hill.

Ginny's eyes looked frantic. "What was that? The engine died while I was driving? How did that happen?" She fumbled with the unfamiliar latch on the door.

Ben hurried out and hustled around to help her out of the car. Then he opened the hood and took a good look at the engine. He didn't have to look far.

"The power output wire that runs from your alternator." He fingered the snapped line, its casings worn through. "Basically, the same wire that snapped on your plane."

"No." Ginny shook her head, the same terrified

expression on her face that Ben had hoped never to see again. "The same wire? So the same person tampered with both engines?"

Unsure what he could possibly say that wouldn't make her more upset, Ben took a couple of steps back from the car, pulling Ginny after him. She hopped unsteadily on her one good foot and leaned against him, her eyes boring into his, looking for answers.

"So this maniac caught up to me? He found me—here, in Holyoake? So fast?"

Ben wished he could tell her otherwise, but the evidence was overwhelming. Still, he felt confused. "We didn't die when the plane crashed. If someone was trying to kill you, why would tampering with your car be more effective than tampering with your plane?"

"It almost was," Ginny corrected him. "If you hadn't grabbed the wheel, I'm sure I would have crashed. Do you think whomever messed with the engine knew I'd sprained my ankle? Maybe they thought I wouldn't be able to get the car stopped without going off the road. Maybe they figured after all I've been through, that I'd freak out and lose it. I would have, if you hadn't been with me."

Unwilling to let her think such pessimistic thoughts, Ben voiced the alternate motive that had occurred to him. "Or maybe they don't necessarily want you dead." Ben looked Ginny straight in the face and watched some of the terror fade from her eyes.

After puzzling over his statement for a moment, Ginny asked, "What do you mean? They just want to injure me? Or scare me?"

Ben looked over to where the hood of the rental car gaped open, the exposed metal of the snapped wire glinting in the sun. "Is there anyone who would have reason to want to scare you—or injure you? Would anyone benefit if you *almost* died?"

Ginny's face bore a thoughtful expression, then she gasped and her hands tightened where they held on to his shirt front. "Get me to a computer. I need to look something up on the internet."

"I'll call Tyler." Much as Ben hated to pull his brother away from his investigative work, Ben hoped Ginny's new insight might provide a break for the case. After a quick phone call to Tyler for a ride, Ben sat on the rental car's rear bumper beside Ginny and tried to get her to open up about her theory.

Her words were vague. "I read something—" she shook her head, clearly frustrated by her inability to recall every detail "—after Kristy's crash. The Dare Divas' stock went up. You know, with Kristy's name in the papers, and everyone realizing that these 'death-defying' stunts we did really were dangerous, people flooded to see our shows. Our posters and T-shirts sold out. We got a *ton* of new endorsement deals."

"So the Dare Divas benefit when one of you gets injured?"

Ginny didn't look convinced. "Maybe. Still, I think I'm worth more as a capable pilot than I would be injured or dead. If somebody was just after the headlines, then why would they target *me?* Why wouldn't they crash a rookie's plane?"

Leaning back against the trunk of the rental car, Ben blew out a long, frustrated breath. "You're the star. You'd get more media attention. And maybe they *didn't* want you injured. Do you think whomever tampered with this engine did it as a warning shot? Maybe they only wanted to scare you."

"Maybe they only wanted to let me know that they know

where I'm hiding." Ginny shivered in spite of the heat of the June afternoon. "But why would they do that? And how did they find me so quickly?"

As Tyler's familiar red Jeep topped the hill, Ben gave Ginny a hand down. "If we could answer that, maybe we could figure out who's after you."

On the way to the airfield office, they filled Tyler in on what had happened. There, Ginny did a quick search of online newspaper archives, and tabbed several relevant articles.

"Read this." She highlighted a disturbing passage for Ben.

The article featured an interview with the Dare Divas' co-owner/manager, Ron Adolph, following Kristy Keller's fiery crash. After offering his condolences toward Kristy's family and his best wishes for her recovery, Ron addressed the question of whether such an accident might ever happen again.

The response chilled Ben's blood as he read Ron's words aloud.

"'Honestly, I'm surprised accidents like this don't happen more often. I've always told our audiences that our girls perform the most dangerous stunts you'll ever see, anywhere. Incidents like this can happen any time. People should come to every one of our air shows. They're all different. You never know when you might witness a crash like Kristy's.'"

Ben couldn't suppress a scowl of displeasure as he reached the end of the quotation.

"What a dirty rat. He used Kristy's accident as an excuse to bring in bigger audiences."

"And it worked." Ginny clicked on another one of the articles she'd tabbed. "Here's an interview with him after the last show we did before heading for Wyoming."

"Public support has been tremendous," Ron Adolph was quoted as saying. "We've sold out every show since Kristy's accident. It's nice to see people rally around the fallen."

"*Nice,*" Ben echoed the word in a tone that said he didn't think Ron's attitude was very nice at all. "Ron's a slippery guy. He says things without really saying them. I don't like the sound of it, but he doesn't give us enough to pin the blame on him, either."

"You're right," Ginny agreed. "He keeps it ambiguous. Maybe there's something there, maybe not. All I know is, I overheard him talking with Earl one day when Earl was complaining about all the reporters messing up his security efforts. Ron said that he'd cut our advertising in half since Kristy's accident. We were getting so much free press he didn't have pay for as much publicity any more."

Ben's hands clenched on the back of her chair and he shook his head, disgusted. "Tyler, are you listening to this?" He called out to his brother, who was across the room, reading pages as fast as they landed in the fax machine tray.

"Ron Adolph," Tyler summarized. "He's got motive, he's got opportunity." He stacked the pages in his hands and carried them over to Ben and Ginny. "He's on my list, along with these suspicious characters." Tyler laid the pages on the desk in front of them.

"Zeke Ward." Ginny read the head mechanic's name off of the top sheet.

"He's wanted in Delaware for failure to pay back child support," Tyler explained. "He was also arrested in conjunction with a grand theft auto charge fifteen years ago, but they didn't have enough evidence to connect him to the crime, and the charges were eventually dropped."

Ben watched Ginny turn back Zeke's page to reveal

information on Doug Adolph. "What did you find on my boss?" she asked.

"On the surface he's squeaky-clean," Tyler admitted, "but he and his brother have had business dealings with several unsavory characters. The deeper I dig, the more I find that I don't like. We're talking big-time crooks here—weapons dealing, embezzlement, white-collar crime. Big names, big players."

"Anyone wanted for murder?" Ginny's voice held an undercurrent of fear.

"Not directly," Tyler qualified, "but then, most of these guys know better than to pull the trigger themselves."

"Ginny," Ben interrupted, "you mentioned earlier that Doug encouraged you to change your name when you first started flying for him. Does he know your real name?" If Doug or his brother knew her real name, they could find out where she was from—which would lead them straight to Holyoake.

Ginny's mouth fell open. "I—I don't know," she stammered, rubbing her temples as though the motion might help her retrieve old memories. "Before I left home after high school, I saw an ad he ran on some aviation websites that said he was looking for stunt pilots. When I arrived in New Jersey to audition, I picked up a packet of information. That's where they first encouraged their pilots to use an alias."

"Did you choose your pseudonym before you applied?" Ben wished he could help her recall all the details.

"Yes." Ginny looked relieved to recall that fact. "I don't think I ever revealed my real identity to Doug and Ron."

"What about your tax withholdings?" Tyler prompted. "Don't they need your real name for that?"

Ginny grinned as she shook her head. "Nope. They

make the checks out to Ginger McAlister. My tax man takes care of the rest."

"Who does your taxes?"

"My brother. He's the only person who knows—" Her smile began to fade.

Ben sensed she'd realized something important. "What? Does someone else know your real name?"

"A few of the guys I dated," Ginny blushed bright red. "But that was years ago."

"Jilted boyfriends." Tyler pulled out a fresh sheet of paper. "I need names, last known address and Social Security numbers if you've got them."

Ben watched as Ginny filled out the information with a trembling hand. He was certain she realized the implications of anyone knowing her real identity. All anyone needed was her real name. From there, they could have easily tracked her back to Holyoake.

After Ginny handed the papers back to Tyler, she continued looking through his pile of suspects, turning the pages and asking in a voice that sounded forcibly light. "What else don't I want to know?" She opened the stack to a page on Earl Conklin. "How's our head of security?"

"I haven't found anything on him."

"I should hope not." Ginny sounded relieved. "I wouldn't think Doug and Ron would hire a security man with a record."

"No." Tyler came around the side of the desk where he could face them both. "I mean I haven't found *anything*— no evidence that he existed more than five years ago."

Ben studied the sparse bit of information the sheet contained on Earl Conklin. "Do you think he changed his name? Ginny, if Doug and Ron asked you girls to fly under stage names, do you think—"

Ginny shook her head. "Earl doesn't perform. Why would he need to change his name?"

"Maybe he has a criminal past." Tyler shrugged and picked up the stack of papers. "I'll keep looking. A lot of your fellow pilots have taken pseudonyms, too."

"You're researching the girls?" Ginny stood.

"Of course." Tyler stared her down. "Girls can be criminals, too."

Ben knew how Ginny felt about investigating the people she trusted. He didn't need to get her started on that argument again. "Don't forget to look for connections to Bobby Burbank," Ben told Tyler. "Obviously he was involved in this somehow."

"I'm on it," the younger McAlister assured his brother as he pulled a set of keys from his pocket. "Did you want to borrow my Jeep to take Ginny home?"

Ben looked at Ginny for the answer. She winced as she tried to step forward on her injured ankle. "I'd appreciate that. If I'm not imposing."

"It's no trouble at all." Ben caught the keys his brother tossed him, then he swept forward and supported Ginny's injured side as she prepared to take another step. "After that, Tyler and I can retrieve your rental car. And maybe tomorrow we can see what we can do about getting your plane back from the sand hills."

When Ginny hobbled silently outside, without protesting or even trying to invite herself along to retrieve the plane, Ben sensed the events of the day had gotten to her. He'd watched as stress etched its way across her face every time his brother had forced her to consider the very people she'd thought she could trust. Nearly every person in her professional support network had been called into question. She'd lost all the people she usually leaned on.

Her slender form rested heavily against him. Ben

wanted so much to pull her close, to offer to replace all those people she could no longer trust. He felt tempted to remind her that she could always come home to Holyoake to stay—that there were plenty of folks in her hometown who'd do everything they could to keep her safe. Especially him.

But, he realized with a pang, that would be taking unfair advantage of the situation. Once the threat against her life was gone, Ginny would go back to Wyoming. It would be unconscionable for him to suggest otherwise, especially knowing how emotionally vulnerable she felt at the moment.

He paused by the door to his brother's Jeep.

"I know you want your freedom—" he began in an apologetic voice.

She held up a hand as though to silence him. "You're not the one who took my freedom from me." She looked up at him with a resigned expression. "You're not the one who should apologize. You've been nothing but helpful. I'm afraid I've made a terrible imposition on your time."

"Nah." Ben dismissed her concern. "We McAlisters live for excitement. Things were getting pretty dull around here."

Her tired smile told him she appreciated his attitude, even if she could have done without the excitement that threatened her life.

Ben's voice grew soft. "I'm just sorry all of these things have happened to you." With his arm still around her shoulder, he had her nearly in a hug, but was still surprised when she leaned closer to him, inching her free hand up around his shoulder as she pulled closer, until they stood nearly nose-to-nose. In all the times he had carried her over the last two days, she'd kept a clear boundary between them.

Now she looked as though there was something more she wanted to express, a simmering hesitancy in her eyes.

He looked down at her, wishing he knew what to say to encourage her. *Stay in Holyoake, where it's safe.* The words were on the tip of his tongue. But how could he speak them, knowing all she'd been through? It wouldn't be fair to her to use her fear against her, to selfishly keep her close to him.

Her lips parted, and he thought for sure she was about to speak.

But the moment slipped away, and she hobbled back, pulling the door open after her.

Ben helped her up into the Jeep.

"Thank you," she said, this time keeping her eyes focused straight ahead.

"No problem." Ben hurried around to the driver's seat and took a deep breath of the fresh Iowa air to clear his thoughts before he climbed in.

They talked amiably about how he planned to get her rental car repaired, and what he and Tyler would try in order to get her downed plane back from the sand hills. But the whole time, Ben wondered about what Ginny had been about to say—or do—earlier.

When they reached the McCutcheon farmhouse, Ben helped her up the stairs. He paused when she reached the front door, and cleared his throat, wanting desperately to ask if there was something…but he didn't have words to ask the question. She thanked him politely and went inside.

Ben trudged back to the Jeep, puzzling over the female mystery behind him. What had she been going to say? Did it have to do with the possible identity of whoever had been after her? That would make sense.

Yes, that had to be it, Ben told himself as he drove back

toward the McAlister airfield. Because the only other possibility that he could think of was that she might have wanted him to kiss her. But that, he was quite sure, was only his own sense of attraction talking. There wasn't any reason for aviatrix Ginger McAlister to be interested in him. For the sake of his own sanity, he needed to remember that.

TEN

Ginny tried to lie low for the next few days while her ankle healed. Her big brother made good on his promise to keep her busy now that she'd given in to his request to return home. She found herself spending time with Cutch and Elise, which made a pleasant excuse for avoiding being with her mother and Bill when they were together. She also got together with Megan, who was on edge about their predicament. She enjoyed seeing her roommate and it also kept her from spending too much time with Ben.

Besides that, Ben had taken off with Tyler to fetch her plane for her, which seemed to be taking longer than they'd hoped, although Ginny imagined they were playing detective, too. She knew Tyler had been eager to see whatever remained of the red dart that had attacked them over the sand hills, and to talk to the investigators who'd found the wreck.

As far as that went, Ginny reminded herself several times over that she was glad for the McAlister brothers' help. When Ben had offered to go back for her plane, she'd tried to assure him he didn't need to, but he'd quickly won that argument. How else was she going to get it back? They'd have to haul it by tractor to the nearest road, and even then, a mechanic would have to fix the engine before the plane could fly again.

And if their help with the plane wasn't enough, the McAlister men seemed determined to get to the bottom of her troubles. Though Ginny couldn't imagine what Tyler's usual rates were, when she'd mentioned payment to Ben when he'd called her to let her know they'd finally gotten her plane out of the sand, Ben had assured her she wasn't expected to pay Tyler anything.

Which made her wonder if Ben wasn't picking up the tab.

That, she told herself as she sat with her injured ankle propped up on her mother's sofa, was ridiculous. She felt deeply indebted to Ben already for all the help he'd provided. In fact, it hadn't escaped her attention that Ben's original assignment had been, as per her brother's request, simply to bring her home in time for the wedding. He'd accomplished that mission. All the hours he'd been putting in on her behalf since then had been out of the goodness of his heart.

Which made her squirm as she sat, foot elevated, switching through the channels on her mother's television. Finally she clicked off the set and leaned back, picturing Ben's handsome face the moment she closed her eyes. She smiled in spite of herself, and felt the tense pain around her heart ease at the mere thought of the man.

Okay, so she liked him. And why shouldn't she? He'd been helpful, and he was fun to be with, even with a murderer on her trail. In fact, she realized as she hugged herself against the cool of the air conditioning, she'd rather trudge through the Great American Desert with Ben at her side than lounge comfortably on a sofa without him.

But that didn't change the fact that she had no business becoming attached to him. She'd liked Kevin, too, but that had only made it so much more difficult for her to move on when she'd finally accepted the fact that she didn't want to live her life for Kevin. She wanted to be her own person.

And the way Ben had chuckled at the idea of Cutch not letting Elise fly her own plane, Ginny knew she didn't want to end up with him. She valued her freedom too much. Which was why she really needed to stop thinking about him all the time. Or at the very least, stop smiling every time his face came to mind.

When the fat tires of the yellow snub-nosed biplane finally touched ground at the McAlister airstrip, Ben eased off the speed and grinned.

He was home. Better yet, he'd brought Ginny's plane home to her. He'd called ahead as he'd neared Holyoake, and Ginny had thanked him profusely, offering to wait for him at the airfield office.

After forcing himself, for safety's sake, to give the yellow bird a thorough post-flight check, he hurried into the office. Ginny sat opposite her bleary-eyed friend Megan Doyle, who leapt up from her chair the moment Ben stepped into the office.

"Do you have any idea what you've done?" Megan demanded, her tone accusatory, her voice raw with emotion.

Completely blindsided, Ben instinctively turned around to make sure Megan wasn't actually talking to someone behind him. Nobody there.

He spun back around to face Megan, who'd advanced toward him and looked like she might try to throttle him if she could get her hands on him. Ben looked to Ginny for help.

Ginny had already jumped up and, moving a little better

on her injured ankle than when he'd left, placed a hand on Megan's shoulder. "He didn't know—"

Megan shook her off. "Then he should have asked. He should have asked me first. Now I don't know what I'm going to do!" Megan buried her face in her hands.

Meeting Ginny's eyes over Megan, Ben mouthed the question, "What did I do?"

Ginny gave him a sympathetic look, but directed her response toward Megan. "Ben and his brother have been trying to help catch whoever's been tampering with the Dare Divas planes—whoever burned our trailer down last week. They needed to do background checks on everyone involved with the Dare Divas—"

"Including me?" Megan looked up imploringly. "Do you really think *I* would do something to hurt you? Do you think I would burn down our trailer? I lost things in that fire, too."

"The background checks." Ben spoke softly, finally understanding what the woman was talking about, even if he was still unclear about why she was so upset. Surely their safety was worth whatever inconvenience the investigation might have caused.

"Yes, the background checks." Megan repeated his words as she glared up at him. "Thanks to you, my ex-husband, who just happens to be my former employer, got a phone call asking whether the Megan Hall who used to work for him isn't the same Megan Doyle who now flies for the Dare Divas." She threw her arms up in the air. "Thank God one of his secretaries was always on my side. She got in touch with the Dare Divas office, got my number and warned me that my new identity was no longer a secret. Otherwise my ex could have kidnapped Noah before I ever knew he'd learned who I was."

Ben felt guilt crumple his stomach into a ball as Megan

spoke. "I'm sorry. I didn't know," he apologized sincerely when she'd finished her story.

"You're right." Megan didn't look satisfied. "You *didn't* know—which is why you should have asked my permission before you investigated me." She grabbed up her purse angrily. "Now I have to check out of the hotel Noah and I checked into using the name Megan Doyle, and I have to figure out a new name and a new place to stay." She marched toward the door, throwing it open before shouting to Ben, "Thanks a lot!"

The door slammed behind her, and she was gone.

It took Ben several moments to digest what had happened and turn to face Ginny. "Where is her son?" He asked Ginny once he'd collected his thoughts enough to speak.

"Your dad is watching him. They seem to get along well."

Ben tried to read whether Ginny was upset with him, too. At least she wasn't shouting. "I had no idea—" he began.

"I know you didn't." Ginny sighed. "I tried to explain to her that you were trying to keep all of us safe—me, Megan and all the Dare Divas. Unfortunately, there was more to the situation than you knew." She walked back to the chair where she'd been sitting, limping only slightly on her sprained side. "Her situation with her ex is complicated. I know he tried to take Noah once before, but that was when they lived in the same town. I have trouble believing he'd go to all the trouble of tracking them down, but Megan insists on taking extreme precautions to protect her son." She shook her head again. "You didn't know all that."

"If I knew everything that was going on, I wouldn't have

such a difficult time catching whoever's after you." Ben sat in the chair opposite Ginny.

"Did you learn anything new on your trip?" Ginny asked, clearly ready to be done talking about the emotional outburst they'd just witnessed.

Though the information he'd gathered now seemed anticlimactic, Ben offered, "The body found in the red dart wreckage has been positively identified as being the same Bobby Burbank who was arrested for attacking you in the hangar last week. Interestingly, it seems our little dogfight caught the attention of a local farmer, who says he saw someone bail out of the plane before it hit the ground."

Ginny's eyes went wide. "You're kidding! That's a lucky break."

"Somewhat. The farmer thought the guy might need some help, so he headed in the direction of where he saw the chute go down."

"And?"

"He never found anyone. Remember, it was pretty well dark out by that time. The farmer came back the next day and found tire tracks. The likely scenario is that the downed pilot called someone to come pick him up during the night."

Ginny shook her head slowly. "An accomplice?"

"It could have been a friend who was unaware of the larger situation. We don't know. Tyler and I went back up to Wyoming and checked into who might have been gone from the Dare Divas team during that time frame. No one knows who took the plane."

"And?"

"It's difficult to say. Most of the girls were around and can vouch for one another. Most of the mechanic's crew were off work and had headed to Gillette. Several of the guys went out together, but not everyone has been accounted for."

"What about Zeke Ward?"

"The guys say he drove into town with a group of them, but there's a good twelve-hour gap of time when nobody saw him."

"Okay." Ginny nodded. "What about Doug and Ron?"

"Doug was a featured speaker at a Wild West Show conference in North Platte, Nebraska. I found a YouTube video of him giving a speech around the same time we were being attacked by the red dart plane. Ron flew down to join him shortly after we left for Iowa. He's in the video helping Doug with his presentation."

Ginny looked relieved to hear that her bosses had good alibis. "And the security crew?"

"I saw their shift rotation. No one was absent for more than twelve hours. When they weren't on duty, they claimed to be eating, sleeping or doing laundry on site."

"Do they have witnesses?"

Ben appreciated the question. "Earl Conklin vouched for them. I guess he runs a pretty tight ship."

"Not tight enough." Ginny shook her head. "Is there anyone who should have been there but wasn't? Any glaring absences?"

Ben felt guilty admitting it after his earlier encounter with Megan, but he knew Ginny needed to hear the whole story. "Megan had a couple of the girls babysit Noah for the night, but nobody knows where she went. She came back early the next morning to get Noah. That's when they left in my plane and came to Holyoake."

Ginny stared at Ben in disbelief. "*Megan?* So she's your top suspect now? What motive could she possibly have had?"

"Jealousy?" Ben's expression softened. "I know you

don't want to think that any of your friends could be behind this, and I don't want Megan to be guilty, either. But we can't disregard her as a suspect."

Little as she liked it, Ginny had to admit Ben had a valid point. "So what do you think we should do?"

"Keep an eye on her," Ben suggested. "She said she needs to find a place to stay. My parents have a big house. They wouldn't mind her staying with them—they already said as much when Tyler told them you had a friend staying at the motel. Why don't we offer to let her stay with my folks? Tyler can keep an eye on her—"

Ginny shook her head the moment Ben mentioned his brother. "I like the rest of the idea, but you should leave Tyler out of it. He's the one who performed the background search on her. She hates him. When she first got here earlier she threatened to kill him."

Ben looked at Ginny meaningfully, and Ginny realized what she'd just said. "I don't think she meant literally. My brother and I used to threaten to kill each other all the time, usually over the last piece of banana bread."

"There's a lot more at stake here than banana bread."

"You're right." Ginny admitted reluctantly after some thought. She'd picked up a new cell phone since she'd been home, and pulled it from her purse. "I'll give Megan a call and tell her about your offer. But I'm not going to mention that Tyler will be there."

Ben smiled as Ginny started to dial, and she felt her stomach do a loop-the-loop. It didn't usually do that when she had both feet on the ground. That's how she knew she wasn't doing a very good job about tamping down her feelings for Ben. She'd just have to try harder, and limit the time she spent with him.

When she closed the call with a tearful Megan, who'd accepted the offer of a place to stay, Ginny blinked down at her phone thoughtfully. "You said whoever bailed out of the red Dare Divas plane probably called for help." She looked up at Ben.

She watched as realization dawned on him, and he glanced back and forth from her phone to her face.

"We didn't have reception in the sand hills." He grimaced, then his eyes brightened once again and he snapped his fingers. "Didn't you say most of the Dare Divas have satellite phones?"

Ginny winced as, with additional names to add to their suspect list, she lost more friends she'd thought she could trust. "Megan and Jasmine both do. Jasmine was one of the girls who met the deputies by my trailer—she and Veronica found Bobby Burbank's rental car." Ginny hated to think her friends might be implicated. She'd trained Jasmine and Veronica. "They're probably not the only ones with satellite phones—just the only two I can recall for sure having them."

"Can you get in touch with some of the girls and try to find out who else might have one?" Ben looked hopeful that the possibility might yield a clue. "Why don't we go down to Nana's Café and catch a burger? We can sort it out over supper."

"Oh." Ginny could feel her face going red at his offer, so she turned her back to him and fumbled around putting her cell phone back in her purse, while she took a couple of deep breaths and thought of an excuse. "I was planning to go shoe shopping. Now that the swelling has gone down on my ankle, I need something to wear besides my old shoes and Veronica's sneaker."

"I wouldn't mind tagging along for the shoe shopping. The shoe store is just down the block from Nana's Café."

Ginny swallowed. Ben didn't mind going shoe shopping with her? That was so sweet. She felt her heart give another little flip, and reminded herself that her attraction to him was all the more reason why she couldn't spend time with him. Hadn't she just resolved not to let her feelings for him get any stronger? "I also need to go clothes shopping," she explained.

"I could—"

"For undergarments," Ginny whispered, as though the word couldn't be spoken out loud in mixed company.

"Oh." Color rose to Ben's cheeks. "Then you don't want me hanging around." He stood and walked over to the computer. "That's fine, then. You can look into the satellite phone possibility on your own time. Just let me know what you find out."

"Sure!" she chirped, a little too brightly. Escaping as far as the door, she remembered her manners. "Thanks for bringing my plane back."

"No problem."

Ginny climbed into the car she'd rented to replace the one that had been tampered with. She felt like dirt. No, lower than dirt. She felt like a worm as she slunk home, ashamed of the way she'd treated Ben. He'd spent two days retrieving her plane, which she knew hadn't been easy, and interviewing folks in connection to the crash. And she couldn't even bring herself to join him at Nana's for a burger?

She was lower than a worm. She was a worm's belly.

There were several cars parked at the McCutcheon house when Ginny arrived, and she entered to find her mother sitting at the kitchen table with Cutch, Elise and Bill. They were all giggling as they pressed molds of cream cheese mints for the wedding reception.

Ginny paused in the doorway. "Did you guys need another hand?"

"We only have four molds." Her mother looked up from

pressing out a rose-shaped candy. "But thanks for your offer."

Bill cleared his throat. "You could join us for dinner later. I'm going to put some steaks on the grill."

"I need to do some shopping." Ginny stuck with the excuse she'd given Ben. Besides, she really did need to buy shoes and clothing after losing hers in the fire.

"That sounds like fun." Elise looked up with a smile.

"Doesn't it?" Anita McCutcheon looked equally intrigued. "I need to get some shapewear before the wedding."

Ginny looked back and forth between her mother and her new sister-in-law. Her excuse about buying undergarments wouldn't work nearly as well with them as it had with Ben. But then, she wasn't necessarily trying to get away from Anita and Elise.

"Maybe—" Anita pressed out another mint "—the three of us girls could go shopping downtown while Cutch and Bill get the grill ready. Then we could all meet at the McAlister place for a late supper."

"I'd love to go shopping with you and Elise," Ginny offered slowly, in the back on her mind dreading the thought of spending time in the company of her mother's boyfriend. It wasn't that she didn't like Bill. She just couldn't stand the thought of being around him and her mother, together. "But Ben already asked me to supper."

"Oh!" Everyone at the table snuck one another knowing glances.

Ginny felt lower than a worm's belly. At the rate she was going, she was going to feel like the center of the earth in no time.

"Then that's the plan." Anita nodded smartly while popping out another mint. "We're almost finished with the mints. Elise and I can run these by the reception hall fridge. Then we girls will go shopping while the boys clean up the kitchen and get the grill ready. The four of us can eat together and Ginny can go on her date with Ben."

"Okay." Ginny felt relieved that at least her mother hadn't tried to invite her and Ben to the barbecue at the McAlisters'. Apparently she thought they needed to be alone for their "date." She headed for the stairs, calling over her shoulder, "I'll just call Ben and let him know what we're up to."

Fortunately, Ginny's stair-climbing skills had been improving along with her healing ankle. She hobbled quickly up to her room and closed the door, throwing herself back onto the bed while wondering how she'd ever gotten herself into this sticky fix. As much as she didn't think she ought to spend time with Ben, there didn't seem to be anything she could do to avoid it—not unless she wanted to spend her evening watching her mom make cozy eyes at Bill. Yuck.

So she'd call Ben, and hopefully he'd understand when she took back her refusal to have dinner with him. Maybe if she was really lucky, he wouldn't read anything into it. After all, when he'd asked it, it had simply sounded as though they were going out to hash over the investigation, not go on a date as her mother supposed.

And then she'd go shopping with her mother and Elise. At least she'd get to spend some more time with her new sister-in-law. They'd have plenty to talk about. Not only did Ginny want to find out why an independent woman like Elise would let Cutch keep her from flying, but Ginny also had to set the record straight with both of the women. They needed to understand that she wasn't going on a date with Ben—that they were just friends, and there was nothing at all romantic between them. After all, if she couldn't convince everyone else of that fact, how would she ever persuade herself to believe she didn't have feelings for him?

Ben flipped through the files he and Tyler had collected on everyone who'd had access to Ginny over the last few weeks. Somewhere in that pile was someone who wanted Ginny dead. Or maybe just seriously injured. Either way, he knew he had to find them and stop them before they succeeded in their efforts.

He couldn't stand the idea that something might happen to her. Granted, from the way she'd struggled to come up with an excuse not to join him for supper, she obviously didn't share the feelings he had for her. Though he'd tried his best to make the invitation sound casual, he knew in his heart of hearts the real reason he'd asked her out. Spending the last two days without her had made him realize how much he missed her, and how much he enjoyed her company when she was around.

Sure, she was going to go back to her stunt-flying troupe as soon as Cutch and Elise's wedding celebration was over. Ben knew that. He didn't have any delusional ideas that he might ever convince her otherwise. But was it too much to ask to spend a little time in her enjoyable company while she was still in Iowa?

Apparently so.

Forcing his mind off Ginny and back onto the reports in front of him, Ben searched for any detail he might have missed, any clue that might point in the direction of one person over another. As he read, he felt the fine hairs at the back of his neck suddenly stand on end. Someone was out there, stalking Ginny, looking for an opportunity to bring her down. It had been three days since Ginny's rental car had been tampered with. Surely her would-be killer was getting ready to strike again.

The ominous feeling grew as Ben flipped through the pages, and he wished Ginny had agreed to let him take her out to dinner. At least then he could keep an eye on her, if only for a short time. He needed to see her, to know that she was okay.

The airfield office phone rang, pulling him from his thoughts. He stood to answer it. "McAlister Airfield, this is Ben."

"Ben."

His heart leapt inside him at the sound of Ginny's voice. Then a shuffling noise behind him caught his attention, and he turned just in time to see an arm swinging something toward his head.

Spinning to the side, he dropped the phone just as a blunt object grazed his temple, half stunning him. He instinctively struck out at his assailant, but the quick-footed attacker leapt back just in time for Ben to see what the man held in his hand.

A gun.

Though his head throbbed from the glancing blow, Ben had enough training in hand-to-hand combat to know how to respond almost on autopilot. He kicked out toward the man's wrist, knocking the gun from his hand.

Now, if only he could see through the blood that streamed down his face from the gash at his temple. Ben tried to get a decent look at his attacker, but the man wore a ski mask that covered everything but his eyes.

His assailant lunged toward where the gun had flown.

Ben threw himself onto the man's back, tackling him and trying to pull the mask off. "Who are you?" He stammered the words as he struggled with the man, who was stronger than Ben had expected.

Or maybe the blow he'd sustained to his head was worse than he thought. Stars flickered on the edges of his vision.

No! He couldn't pass out now, not when he was so close to catching whoever was after Ginny.

But the man in the mask jerked backward with his elbow, catching Ben hard just below the ribs, and sending anger searing through him along with the pain. No way was he going to let this guy get the best of him.

He blocked the man's next couple of blows and got him with a pretty hard knock to the jaw before the man's leg swept out in a swift kick, a little too fast for Ben's pain-dulled senses to anticipate.

His legs went out from under him and he lunged forward as he dropped, pulling his attacker down onto the polished cement floor of the airfield office. The man hit the floor with a satisfying thud.

Ben scrambled up just in time to see his attacker's hand reach for the gun.

"Stop investigating me," the attacker demanded, pointing the gun at Ben. He pulled the trigger, and Ben flinched as a sharp pain sliced through his gut.

"It's none of your business anyway." The man's cold laughter echoed through the metal building. His foot flew forward and he caught Ben's face in a harsh kick before he fled away. "That will teach you to keep your nose out of other people's business."

Clutching his injured midriff, Ben fought against the darkness that seemed intent on swallowing him.

The phone. He had to get to the phone. Ginny had been on the phone. Maybe, if she was still on the line, he could talk to her. He could get her to call for help.

Rolling onto his side, he tried to sit up. But the pain was too much and the darkness too heavy. "Help," he gasped, his voice faint, even to his own ears.

But there was no help. There was only darkness.

ELEVEN

Ginny hobbled down the stairs as fast as her injured foot would carry her, and nearly stumbled twice in her haste. She had her cell phone to her ear, though all she could hear were the sounds of struggle. Ben had shouted, "Who are you?" which told Ginny that whomever he was fighting with had no business being in the airfield office, and probably no business being in Holyoake, either. She could hear scrambling noises—it sounded like he was fighting with someone.

There was no one in the kitchen. Ginny could have kicked herself for taking her time working up the courage to call Ben. Now her mother and brother had left with Bill and Elise, and Ginny didn't have anyone to help her. And she wasn't about to hang up the phone on Ben to call anyone else. Nor would she take the time to use the landline phone. She couldn't drive and use the home phone at the same time.

And she had to get to the airfield—*fast*. It was only a couple of miles away.

Lunging outside on her one good foot, she leapt into her rental car and sped away, caring little that the gravel roads of rural Holyoake County weren't made for speed.

The scrambling noises that had echoed through the

phone on her lap now ceased, and Ginny wondered what was going on. Had the connection cut out?

Then a harsh voice demanded, "Stop investigating me," and an impossibly loud shot sounded.

Ginny jumped at the sound and pressed her foot down further on the accelerator.

"Please God," she prayed, "don't let Ben be hurt. Please let him be okay." She held the wheel steady with one hand while she picked up the phone and held it to her ear. With a gasping breath, she spoke into the phone, "Ben?"

She topped the next hill and listened intently, keeping the phone to her ear and her eyes on the road. Silence. Even the sounds of struggle had ceased. And then faintly, so faintly she might have almost thought she imagined it, she heard a weak voice whisper, "Help."

Dust flew as Ginny slid her speeding rental car to a stop in front of the airfield office, taking out a row of cheery marigolds in the process. Oops. She'd have to remember to apologize to Elise about those later.

Diving in the front door and ignoring the stab of pain from her ankle, she recoiled at the sight of blood on the floor. "No!" she screamed, rushing forward to find Ben in a pool of red.

She threw herself down and fumbled at his neck. Jugular, where was the jugular? Shouldn't he have a pulse somewhere?

There. It didn't feel particularly strong, but he had one.

Realizing he needed help *now,* Ginny snapped her phone shut, found the airfield phone where it dangled from the desk nearby, and slammed it back onto its receiver, effectively cutting off the connection from the call she'd placed earlier. Then she popped open her phone and dialed 911, quickly relaying the situation.

While she spoke to the emergency operator, Ginny

favored her re-wrenched ankle and half crawled back across the floor toward Ben, lifting his shoulders gently, scooping his head onto her lap.

"Emergency vehicles are on their way," the dispatcher's voice assured her.

"Thank you. Tell them to hurry." She wiped off some of the blood from Ben's face, which appeared to be coming mostly from a wicked-looking gash near his temple.

"Oh, Ben." She kissed the spot on his forehead she'd just wiped clean. "Ben, stay with me. Please."

But Ben didn't seem to hear her. Ginny pinched her eyes shut as pain tore through her heart. It wasn't that same stress-induced sting she'd felt before Ben had walked into her life. No, this was a horrible ache that touched a deeper part of her heart.

She'd given up on praying when God had let her father die. But now she had nowhere else to turn. "Please, Lord," she begged, holding Ben's head on her lap, "don't let Ben die. *Please* don't let Ben die." She gulped back her tears and pressed her forehead to Ben's.

Sirens in the distance caught her attention. Good. The Holyoake hospital was on the edge of town closest to the airfield. They didn't have far to go. Ginny's fingers felt for the spot where she'd last found Ben's pulse. There was something still beating there, but it felt so faint she couldn't stand it.

"Come on, hurry!"

With one final kiss on Ben's forehead, she gently laid him back down on the floor and, wincing against the pain of her injured ankle, pushed a couple of chairs out of the way to make a clear path from the door to where Ben lay, then hurried to open the door for the paramedics.

Dead Reckoning

The ambulance came to a stop next to her rental car.

"Here! He's in here!" she shouted as the medics jumped out.

While the crew got to work on Ben, Ginny stayed back, watching and wondering what each action meant. Much as she wanted to ask if they thought he'd be okay, she didn't want to interrupt them. Surely every second counted.

Soon Ben was loaded onto a gurney, with tubes dangling around him and an oxygen mask over his face.

A paramedic turned to her. "Did you want to ride in with us?"

"Yes, please." She followed them and tried not to get in the way as they settled into the back of the ambulance. "It is okay if I hold his hand?"

The nurse nearest her smiled. "Go ahead, honey."

"Thanks." Ginny sniffled and picked up the big, calloused hand that had supported her so strongly over the last week. Unable to stand the sight of his face so pale beneath his tanned skin, she pinched her eyes shut and continued to pray silently that Ben would be all right after all.

When they reached the Holyoake hospital, Ginny reluctantly let go of his hand. As they pushed him away through a set of double doors, past a sign that read *authorized personnel only*, Ginny held back uncertainly.

"There's a waiting room down the hall," the friendly EMT told her, "and a restroom if you want to get cleaned up."

Ginny found the restroom and recoiled at her appearance. Ben's blood covered the front of her shirt. How could he lose so much of it and still be okay? Pinching back a sob, she started scrubbing her hands at the sink, and nearly had the red out from under her fingernails when the ring of her cell phone surprised her.

Reality came back. Oh, yes, her mom was probably wondering where she was. Ginny glanced at the time before answering the call. Yup, she was supposed to have met her mom and Elise at a downtown shop ten minutes ago. And a thoughtful person probably would have called Ben's folks by this time.

"Hello?" Ginny answered the phone. The laughter in the background told her Elise was nearby, and apparently no one knew about what had happened at the airfield.

Her mom rattled on, something about the sale prices and that Ginny should get there before she and Elise bought out the store. More giggling.

Ginny took a deep breath. Oh, what should she tell them? What could she say? She'd already stretched the truth enough that day.

"Ginny?" Anita McCutcheon paused in her animated story. "Are you still there?"

"Something happened to Ben, Mom. We're at the hospital."

"What? What happened? Are you okay?"

"I'm fine." She looked at her ruined clothes in the mirror. "Can you bring me a fresh outfit? And call Ben's folks. I'm at the lounge near the emergency room."

"I know it well. We'll get there as soon as we can."

Ginny realized her mom probably knew the hospital backward and forward after all the years her father had been sick. "Thanks, Mom."

"Is Ben going to be all right?"

"I don't know." Ginny fought back a vicious lump in her throat. "I hope so."

"We'll be there soon."

"Thanks. 'Bye." Ginny closed the phone and finally let her suppressed tears fall. *Would* Ben be okay? She'd never forgive herself if he wasn't. After all, she'd heard enough of the attack over the phone to know without a doubt that it was all her fault.

*That will teach you to keep your nose out of other peo-
ple's business.* She should never have let Ben get involved
in her troubles. She should never have let him bring her
home to Holyoake. Now whoever was after her was among
them threatening the people she loved.

With her hands and face clean and nothing more to do
but wait until her mom arrived with fresh clothes, Ginny
hobbled toward the waiting room, where the sight of an
imposing man in uniform made her want to shrink back
around the corner, out of sight.

But the sheriff had already seen her.

"Ginny McCutcheon?" He extended his hand.

"Yes." She answered reluctantly and wished that her
hand wouldn't tremble so much as she shook his.

"I'm Sheriff Gideon Bromley. I'd like to ask you some
questions about what happened at the airfield office."

"Um, okay." Ginny looked down at her blood-covered
shirt and tried to think. The sheriff probably considered
her a suspect in the attack on Ben. Well, she certainly had
enough blood on her shirt to make her look guilty. "Can
we sit down?" What with all her scrambling to help Ben,
she'd wrenched her sprained ankle again, and it was throbbing.

"Sure." Sheriff Bromley led her to a bank of chairs in
the waiting area which, to Ginny's relief, was completely
unoccupied. Unlike the New Jersey waiting room after
Kristy's accident, which had been swarming with people,
the small-town hospital wasn't terribly busy as evening approached.

As Ginny relayed the events to the sheriff, she struggled
to recall everything as it had happened in order. Her concerns about Ben muddied her thoughts. How long would it
be before she learned how he was doing? How badly was
he hurt?

"And the reason for your phone call?" the sheriff asked.

"Huh?" Ginny tried to tear away her mind from the fears that weighed it down.

"You said you called the airfield office and overheard the attack over the phone." The sheriff read from his notes. "What prompted your phone call to the airfield?"

"Oh." Ginny blushed. Why did this have to be so complicated? If she hadn't looked guilty before, she probably did now. "Ben had asked me earlier if I'd like to go to dinner with him, and I turned him down. I was calling back to let him know I changed my mind."

"Ah." Sheriff Bromley nodded and began writing again.

Ginny wondered if the *ah* was an I-think-she's-guilty sort of *ah* or an innocent *ah*. She didn't know enough about law enforcement to tell the difference.

Through the wide glass doors of the waiting room entrance she saw her mother and Elise approaching. The doors slid open automatically.

"There you are!" Her mother's familiar squeal of relief brought Ginny to her feet. For a moment she thought her mom was going to hug her, but Anita McCutcheon's eyes went wide at the sight of all the blood on Ginny's shirt. "I thought you said you were okay?"

"I am." Ginny explained. "This is Ben's blood."

Elise, who had come hurrying in on Anita's tail, yelped as she came to a halt. "That's Ben's blood? What happened?"

Ginny looked at the sheriff. "Can I tell them?"

"That's up to you," he responded, his posture telling her that he intended to stay and listen to whatever she said.

With a gulp, Ginny started to rehash the whole thing for her mother and Elise. When she reached the part where she heard the loud shot over the phone, Elise covered her mouth.

"He was *shot?*"

The reality of her words nearly caused Ginny to crumple on the spot. "I—I guess so. There was all that blood."

"Where was he shot? Is he going to be okay?" Elise continued on, her expression almost frantic.

Movement behind the wide glass door caught Ginny's eye, and she watched the doors slide open again. "There you are!" Cutch and Bill waved at the women from the doorway, and hurried over to join them.

"What happened?" Cutch asked his little sister. "You look awful."

"Ben was shot." Elise took her husband's arm.

While Elise hurriedly caught Bill and Cutch up on what had happened, Ginny stood by, dazed, struggling to answer their questions while her thoughts were mostly on Ben. Her presence in Holyoake had nearly killed him. She had to leave as soon as Cutch and Elise's wedding celebration was over in four days. Could she make it four more days? Could Ben?

The sheriff listened to their chatter awhile longer, than excused himself, heading down another hall of the hospital. Ginny wished she could follow him and find where they'd taken Ben. She couldn't stand waiting to find out if he was going to be okay. If he was going to live.

"So what does the sheriff think?" Cutch asked once the man had exited.

Everyone looked at Ginny as though expecting her to answer. "I don't know. He probably thinks *I* did it. I'm the one covered in blood."

"Gideon Bromley will handle your case fairly," Cutch predicted. "He's learned not to jump to conclusions." Cutch gave Elise a meaningful look.

Elise grinned. "Oh, yes, he's a great sheriff. And a nice guy. He was married last winter and now his wife is expecting a baby. They're in our—"

"Elise." Cutch's tone was chastising, and he gave his wife a scolding look.

"Oh!" Elise's eyes went wide. "Sorry to babble. We brought you clothes, Ginny. Want to go change?"

"Thank you." Ginny took the bag of clothes her mother and Elise had brought from the downtown shop where she had been supposed to meet them earlier. But as she hobbled toward the restroom to change, she couldn't help but feel irked by the way Cutch had so abruptly silenced Elise. Sure, she'd always thought he was bossy when they were little, but he was her big brother. He was supposed to be bossy to her. He wasn't supposed to boss Elise around.

Was that the kind of behavior Ben and Tyler had chuckled over in the plane? Did they think it was funny to see someone bossing their cousin around?

Ginny didn't like it. She wondered if she'd get a chance to ask Ben about it.

In the mean time, she changed clothes and folded up her bloodied garments in the shopping bag. Would the sheriff want them as evidence? She had no idea. She was in way over her head.

She hobbled back out toward the waiting room, rounding the corner just in time to see Ben's parents, Leroy and Linda McAlister, as they approached the clear glass doors of the waiting area.

Ginny quickly ducked back behind the corner.

How could she face them? Ben's injuries were completely her fault. They probably hated her. Even if it hadn't been for that stupid feud that had gone on between their families—even if, as Ben had told her days before, the McCutcheons and McAlisters got along well these days—that didn't change the fact that Ben had been injured because of her. That he might die because of her.

Unable to muster up the courage to approach them, Ginny instead headed back down the hospital hallway, away from the waiting area. She had no idea where she was going, but she had to get away from Leroy and Linda. Eventually she'd have to face them, but not yet, not until she got a handle on her emotions. Her ankle throbbed as she hobbled down the carpeted hall.

Just when she'd begun to think she couldn't go another step on the aching ankle, Ginny found a room marked "Chapel." She peeked inside and, seeing no one in the evening light that streamed through the west-facing stained glass window, she ducked into a pew near the back.

The faint notes of a hymn tinkled pleasantly. As Ginny recalled from visits to the hospital when her father was ill, the music was piped in from somewhere, probably meant to soothe those who'd come to the chapel for refreshment. She recognized the tune to the old hymn "Softly and Tenderly," and her mind supplied the words to fit the notes.

"Softly and tenderly Jesus is calling, calling for you and for me. Come home, come home. You who are weary, come home."

She looked up at the image of Jesus in the stained glass window, with a sheep over his shoulders and a few more sheep at his feet. *Come home, come home. You who are weary, come home.*

The sound of a clearing throat caught Ginny's attention, and she turned to find Leroy McAlister standing in the aisle.

"Mind if I sit?"

The last thing Ginny wanted to do was explain to Leroy how Ben had been injured, or to have to admit to Ben's father that his injury was all her fault. But she couldn't run away now. Ducking her head, she silently slid over to make room for him.

The big man eased himself into the pew.

He sat in silence for a few moments, and Ginny braced herself for his anger. Leroy McAlister was known to have a temper. He'd once pulled a rifle on Cutch.

"I've always liked that window." Leroy pointed to the image of Jesus at the front of the chapel.

Ginny took a deep breath and tried to formulate a response. But between her fears for Ben and her fear of Leroy, the best she could muster was a soft, "Yeah."

"The Bible says that whenever one of the sheep wanders off, the shepherd will leave the rest of the flock to find the missing sheep." He gestured with a work-worn, tanned hand to the elaborate window. "See how Jesus carries the lamb over his shoulders like that?"

"Mm-hmm." Ginny sniffled. "Why does he do that? Doesn't the lamb get heavy? Or scratchy?" She thought about how scratchy some of her wool sweaters felt. She couldn't imagine carrying a live, wriggly sheep on her shoulders.

"Sometimes when sheep wander off, they get hurt. If a sheep breaks a leg, the shepherd won't just leave him behind. But he's vulnerable on his own like that, and the wolves or lions might pick him off."

"So the shepherd carries him?" Ginny risked a glance at Ben's dad and saw his lips twitching with emotion. He appeared to be blinking back tears. She had a feeling this story meant something.

"The shepherd carries the sheep until he heals." Leroy cleared his throat. "Do you know why Ben finally retired from the Air Force?"

"Why?"

Leroy shook his head. "You ask him."

Ginny's mouth fell open. She only prayed she'd get the opportunity to ask Ben that question—to talk to Ben again at all. "Is he going to be okay?"

"I don't know. I suppose I ought to go check and see if anybody knows anything yet."

After Leroy left, Ginny spent a long time looking up at the stained-glass Jesus and puzzling over everything Leroy had said. She still didn't know if the man was upset with her. Maybe he was waiting to find out if Ben was going to recover before he decided whether to be furious with her.

And what did he mean by his story about the shepherd and the lamb? Was he trying to tell her something? If so, Ginny wasn't sure what it was.

As she sat, Ginny found herself praying inside her head. Sure, God had let her down when He took her father away from her. But God was the only One Ginny knew who had control over life and death. Ginny had already let Ben down by luring a vicious criminal to Holyoake. She wasn't about to let him down again by not praying. She folded her hands and begged God to heal Ben.

When she looked up, the fading light outside no longer illuminated the details of the window. All she could see was Jesus and the lamb, and she felt a pang deep in her heart, a pain that sliced right through all the hurt she'd felt in the past few weeks, and even the past few months since her father's death.

Recalling what life had been like before her father's illness, Ginny wished it was possible to turn back the clock to those carefree days. "I wish I could go home," she whispered. But even as she spoke the words, she chided herself. Home would never be the same again.

The sun had sunk and darkness had claimed the room when Tyler entered the chapel. "There you are. Ben's asking for you."

Relieved to hear Ben was up to speaking, Ginny hurried to follow Tyler to the room where Ben was recovering from surgery. As Tyler explained it, everyone else, including the sheriff, had already talked to Ben. Now he wanted to see her. After all she'd done—sending him after her plane, turning down his offer for dinner and ultimately provoking the attack on his life, she couldn't imagine what he wanted to see her for.

TWELVE

Ben felt tired. Drained. Well, after losing so much blood, he figured he probably had a right to feel drained.

Tyler ducked his head inside the door. "We're heading home for the night. You get some rest."

"Thanks." Ben didn't even try to raise his hand to wave at his brother. He was too exhausted. Besides, he felt a little disappointed, not so much that his family was leaving him, but that Ginny still hadn't been by. He'd asked about her, but no one seemed to know where she might be, and Ben didn't want to sound like he was overly desperate to see her. Even if he was.

When Ginny entered the room a moment later, Ben couldn't resist grinning. "You changed your mind about dinner?"

But instead of smiling back, Ginny's face looked drawn. She seemed hesitant as she approached him. "I'm sorry you got hurt. I'm sorry I turned you down for dinner. I was actually calling to tell you I changed my mind."

"That's what the sheriff said."

Ginny's eyes brightened. "Does he have any idea who attacked you?"

"A guy." Ben would have shrugged if he hadn't been bandaged so tightly. "A big guy."

"Not Megan."

"Nope, we can rule her out, along with that Zeke guy. I didn't ever get a look at his face, but the man who attacked me was definitely bigger than Zeke."

Ginny felt glad that her friend was off the hook. "And he said, 'stop investigating *me*.' So it wasn't a hired attack, then. Whoever's been after me and the other Divas came by himself."

"You heard what my attacker said?" Ben coughed. Even his lungs felt weak, and talking required effort. "Over the phone?"

"Yes." Ginny's eyes softened and she picked up his hand where it lay at his side. "I heard the whole attack. I was so worried for you. When I heard that shot—" Her voice broke off.

"Don't worry about it." Ben wished he could pull her into a hug, but it was all he could do to keep talking. "I'm just glad you heard what was happening and found me when you did." He didn't like the way she looked like she was going to cry just thinking about the attack, so Ben brought the conversation back to the hunt for the attacker.

"I need to look back over all the folks we've been investigating." He outlined the next step in the search. "If we can go through and rule out all the women and smaller-framed men, that will narrow our field. That puts us down to the men who work for the Dare Divas, and those guys you dated in the past."

"Did you learn anything about them?"

"A couple of the guys have records."

Ginny let go of Ben's hand to cover her face. "How embarrassing."

Ben immediately missed her touch, but reminded himself that he had no claim to her. He would never have any claim to her. "Sorry I didn't tell you sooner. I haven't seen much of you, and the investigation has been moving quickly."

"It's okay." Ginny uncovered her face. "I appreciate all you've done, really. And I feel so horrible about what happened. I wish there was some way I could make it up to you."

For an awkward instant, Ben considered declaring his love for her. He could tell her that one kiss would make up for everything. But, he chastised himself, he couldn't manipulate her feelings like that. He couldn't ask her to love him just because she felt guilty that he'd been shot.

Besides, he knew how much she loved flying and how much she loved the wide, blue, open sky. So even if he ever thought, in his wildest dreams, that she might be interested in him, he could never ask her to settle down and leave her career behind. She was too wild a creature to ever be happy with him.

Ginny continued, "I don't know how I can face your folks. Your dad tried to talk to me in the chapel earlier. I was terrified."

"Why?"

"Because it's all my fault. I brought this madman to Holyoake. If it hadn't been for me, you would never have gotten shot." She looked at the ceiling and appeared to consider something. When she looked down at him again, her question surprised him. "Why did you retire from the Air Force?"

Ben chuckled painfully, his midriff aching near where the bullet had taken out his spleen. At least he'd been hit in something relatively disposable. "I broke my leg."

"In combat?" Ginny gasped.

"Nope. Playing football with some of the guys. But it made me stop and think. I entered the military because I wanted to be a hero. But I never got wounded in battle. I got hurt playing games. I think God had been trying to tell me to come home for a while, but He finally got my attention. Life is about more than being a hero. It's about being with the people we love." He shook his head. "I don't know if I explained that very well."

But Ginny's blue eyes looked down at him tenderly. "I think you explained it perfectly." She touched his hand. He wanted to entwine her fingers in his, to hold her hand again, but he felt so exhausted, a dragging kind of exhaustion that pulled him relentlessly toward sleep.

"I should let you get your rest."

Ben managed half a smile. "Thanks for stopping by. Come see me again."

"I'll try," Ginny promised as she hurried out.

As her red hair disappeared down the bend of the hallway, Ben felt a little part of his heart go with her.

Ginny resolved to lie low until the wedding. Hopefully with Ben in the hospital, his investigation indefinitely suspended, her attacker would realize no one was hunting him right now. Maybe they'd get lucky and he'd just go away.

Even when Tyler tried to get together with her to go over the list of suspects again, Ginny turned him down. Pursuing her attacker only led to more attacks. Hadn't the man said as much just before he'd shot Ben? Besides, she knew there were still too many large-framed men in the pile of possibilities to even begin to narrow the field to a workable number.

Perhaps most importantly, she didn't want Tyler working on the case any more because she didn't want him getting hurt, too. Since Tyler was the professional investigator, Ginny felt a little surprised that Ben had been attacked instead of his little brother. But, she realized with another gut punch of guilt, she didn't have the same feelings for Tyler. By injuring Ben, her attacker had dealt yet another blow to her. She didn't know how her adversary knew about her feelings for Ben, but there was no doubt in her mind that his target had been deliberate.

Getting close to her had nearly cost Ben his life, just as Kristy Keller being her friend and coworker had caused Kristy's accident. There was nothing she could do to go back in time and change things. All she could do was keep a low profile for three more days, and then leave as soon as the wedding was over.

And pray she didn't get shot in the meantime. Though praying had felt futile ever since her father's death, she'd realized when Ben was shot that she needed God's help, even if she didn't always like the way He allowed things to turn out. She couldn't see *how,* but she prayed earnestly that God would heal the situation she was in, and keep them all safe from danger for a few more days.

Ginny also decided it would be okay to spend time with Megan again. Since the attacker was obviously a man, Megan was innocent. And Ginny felt she owed it to her friend to at least try to make up to her the fact that the investigation had given away her new identity.

So between shopping for the clothes and shoes that she still had never been to the store to buy, and the inevitable dress fitting that Ben had threatened her with when he'd first arrived in Wyoming, Ginny had a full plate of activities.

She almost managed to not miss Ben so much, even though she thought about him constantly as he lay in his hospital bed, recovering. Since she'd promised him she'd come for a visit, she made sure to stop by every day, but only when someone else was with her. She wasn't sure her heart could take much more time with him alone.

So she had Megan and Noah in tow when she went to visit him two days before the big wedding celebration.

"The doctor has good news," Ben announced with a smile. The color had begun to return to his face and he no longer looked like he might pass out at any moment. Ginny was glad for that.

"Oh?" she asked eagerly.

"If I take it easy and rest up here today, he says I can go home tomorrow, and be in the wedding celebration the day after that."

"That's excellent!" Ginny hadn't realized how much she wanted to see him standing on his own two feet before she left Iowa for good. "I'd have to give you a hard time if you missed it, after all you went through to bring me back in time."

Ben smiled at her, his streaky hazel eyes warm. "I couldn't give up my spot and let somebody else walk you down the aisle."

"Oh!" Ginny sputtered as an image popped into her mind of Ben on her arm, and her face under a veil. Ben was going to walk her down the aisle? Fortunately, Noah chose that moment to interrupt and ask questions about the machines that surrounded Ben, so Ginny got a few seconds to recover without all the attention focused on her.

After her initial surprise, Ginny realized what Ben must be referring to. She was a bridesmaid, which meant she'd be processing in ahead of the bride. And though she'd never thought to ask who it would be, she realized now she'd have a man escorting her in.

Ben.

Ginny tried to keep up with Noah's active chatter, but her heart was beating as though she'd been chased. Okay, so she was going to walk down the aisle with Ben. No big deal. It meant nothing. People were in weddings together all the time. She'd do it for Cutch and Elise.

She'd just have to redouble her efforts not to give away her feelings. It would only be a short time, and then, as soon as the celebration was over, she'd head for Wyoming, and take all the danger away with her.

As Ginny and Megan exited the hospital, Ginny's thoughts were still with Ben. Maybe that's why she didn't see the familiar figure approaching them until he stood immediately in front of her.

"Ginger!" Doug Adolph exclaimed. "And Megan!" The owner of the Dare Divas stunt flying troupe stepped forward and wrapped Ginny in a big hug.

Shocked at Doug's sudden appearance on her home turf, Ginny took a second to recover from her surprise at seeing the man to whom she owed her successful career. Something about the situation didn't seem right.

Doug pulled back and took Ginny by her shoulders. "I've been so worried about you. Earl tells me there was an attack? A friend of yours was shot?"

"Yes." Ginny hurried to update Doug on all that had happened. She noticed he didn't make any sort of move to embrace Megan. Well, that only made sense. Megan had her hands full holding Noah. And Doug had long been like a father to Ginny, mentoring her during the early years of her career.

His familiar silver hair rippled in the breeze as Doug shook his head. "I shouldn't have let you out of my sight. We haven't had any incidents in Wyoming since you left. I think you should return to the training grounds immediately. Earl has hired increased security. You'll be safer there."

Ginny was glad her boss felt that way, and tried to quash her feelings that something was wrong. "I will. Two days from now, in fact. My brother's wedding celebration is Saturday afternoon. I'll show my face at the reception afterward and then sneak away."

"Good." Doug looked relieved. He addressed both Ginny and Megan. "I want both of you girls in the cockpit on Monday. We've got new segments to practice. I'm planning to move ahead with the summer tour at the end of June. We'll hit the state fair circuit like we always do."

"Do you think it's safe?" Ginny asked.

"Oh, Ginger." Doug gave her a sympathetic look. "We're never truly safe, are we? We take too many risks for that. But I think we need to stay one step ahead of this madman. If we move fast he won't be able to keep up. Besides, Earl tells me this private investigator of yours, this Tyler McAlister, thinks he's on to something."

"When did Earl talk to Tyler?" Ginny wasn't even aware Tyler was still pursuing the case after she'd told him not to. She thought he'd backed down after the attack on his brother.

"Oh, they're on the phone several times a day. Earl is constantly talking to the investigators—in Wyoming, Nebraska, even your local sheriff. He's staying on top of everything. He's determined to keep you safe."

As the man spoke, Ginny finally focused her scattered thoughts on just what was bothering her. "How did you know where to find me?" Other than Megan, she hadn't revealed her whereabouts to anyone associated with the Dare Divas.

"Earl told me where you were."

The news surprised Ginny, but then, she realized that if Earl had been talking with local authorities, her whereabouts must have eventually become obvious. She wondered if Tyler or Ben considered the breach of information to be of concern. Apparently not.

Walking more steadily on her healing ankle, Ginny led the way as they made their way across the parking lot to where Ginny and Megan had parked Ginny's rental car.

Her thoughts still swirling with what other information Tyler and Earl might have exchanged, Ginny recalled Tyler mentioning that he hadn't found any record of Earl's existence more than five years back.

She smiled at Doug. "Remember when I started flying for the Dare Divas and we first started doing air shows?"

"Yes." Doug nodded, happy memories alight in his smile.

"You and Ron encouraged us all to take stage names," she continued. "I'm glad for that. I think it's helped me stay ahead of trouble in the past, although obviously whoever's been after me lately knows who I really am."

"Do you think so?" Doug looked concerned.

Ginny continued. "Did anyone else take on another name? I mean, besides the girls who fly?"

Doug looked thoughtful.

"Did Earl Conklin ever go by another name?"

Doug's eyes lit up, and he tipped his head back, chuckling. "You figured that one out, did you? Ha ha! I'll have to tell Earl. Or shall I say, Allen. He thinks he can out-wit everyone." Doug paused in his chuckling. He must have seen the concern on Ginny's face, because he spoke reassuringly.

"Oh, Ginger, you don't have to worry about Allen, or Earl, or whatever you want to call him. Yes, he changed his name, but only because he needed a fresh start after some awkward brushes with the law during his younger years. But you can trust him completely."

Ginny was glad for Doug's reassurances, even if it bothered her that Earl really had been hiding a secret past all this time. "How can you be so certain?"

Doug's eyes twinkled with amusement. "Because Earl Conklin's real name is Allen Adolph. He's my son."

Ginny was glad to find Tyler at his parents' house when she stopped to drop off Megan and Noah. She waited for Megan to stomp past him—she still wasn't talking to Tyler after the background check—and then she joined him where he sat eating a fat wedge of watermelon on the front porch steps.

"Melon?" Tyler offered, cutting another slice off the perfectly ripe fruit that sat on the cutting board beside him.

"Thanks." Ginny took the juicy slice and sat near him. After enjoying a few bites of the tasty fruit, she asked the question on her mind. "Did Earl ever tell you he had an alias?"

Tyler shot a few watermelon seeds from his mouth into some nearby bushes. "Nope. When I couldn't find anything by digging, I came out and asked him point-blank why there was no record of Earl Conklin more than five years ago. He just laughed it off and told me to stick to the relevant parts of the case."

"So you don't consider him a suspect?"

"I consider anyone who's been anywhere near you a suspect—and I'm not even going to narrow it down to big guys like Ben thinks. We already know there's an accomplice. The tire tracks in Nebraska prove that."

"So who are your top suspects?"

Tyler made a face. "A couple of your old boyfriends were pretty shady characters. I haven't ruled out Zeke Ward, either. And your fellow pilots are still a concern. I've been keeping an eye on Megan."

"Megan?" Ginny whispered, afraid her friend might overhear, even from inside the house. "Why?"

"She sure knows how to hold a grudge, for one thing." Tyler looked less than pleased about that fact. "I'm just not sure we can trust her."

Ginny munched a few more bites of watermelon thoughtfully. "Doug Adolph trusts Earl."

"I know." Tyler hacked another slice off the melon. "And Earl has been more than cooperative getting me any information I ask for. That's why I haven't been too worried about him. But I sure would like to know his alias, just the same."

Ginny finished her watermelon slice and stood. "It's Allen Adolph. Earl is Doug's son."

"I wonder if that connection means anything." Tyler spit a few seeds toward the bushes.

"If Doug thought Earl had anything to hide, he wouldn't have told me his alias. It's not like I twisted his arm. He volunteered the information." Ginny waved as she headed for her rental car. "Thanks for the watermelon."

As she hurried away, Ginny thought about what Tyler had been able to tell her. Precious little. They still had no definite leads on who had been after her, which was all the more reason why she had to get out of town as soon as she could. They were no closer now to nabbing the guilty party than they had been when Ginny had arrived in Holyoake. But the danger and the threat to her loved ones had drawn closer than ever.

Ginny stopped by the next day to see Ben, and was surprised to discover him sitting at the edge of the bed, fully dressed except for his shoes, which sat next to him on the hospital bed.

He looked up and grinned at her as she came in. "Hey, Ginny." His voice was still weak, though much of the color had returned to his face.

"Are you going home?" She noticed he was no longer connected to an IV.

Ben nodded. "As soon as I can muster up the strength to get my shoes on and find someone to drive me home."

"I can drive you home," Ginny volunteered, realizing only after she said it that the last time they'd been in a car together, things hadn't gone well. "I can help you get your shoes on, too."

"That would be great. I can't believe I'm so exhausted after getting dressed. And bending over to reach my feet puts a strain on my stitches."

Ginny made a face at that idea. "Don't do anything to strain your stitches." The doctors had explained that, after removing Ben's spleen and repairing some blood vessels and sections of intestine that had been sliced by the bullet, they'd left behind hundreds of internal stitches that would dissolve once his injury had healed. But in the meantime, he was at risk of internal bleeding if he pulled the stitches.

She took the shoe he handed her and worked it onto his foot for him. "If you reinjure yourself they won't let you out of here after all."

"That's what I'm afraid of."

With Ginny's help, Ben soon had both feet tied into his sneakers and was ready to go. A nurse insisted on pushing him in a wheelchair to the front door, even though Ginny could tell Ben wasn't happy about being treated like an invalid.

Her father hadn't ever liked that treatment, either, the many times she'd accompanied him to the hospital for chemotherapy. The sights and smells of the hospital brought back the memories she'd worked so hard to suppress.

Ginny pulled up to the carport and helped Ben ease himself into the passenger seat. Fortunately the second car she'd rented was even roomier than the one that had been tampered with, so there was plenty of room for Ben's large frame.

As she drove, Ben gave directions on how to find his place. "You know that old McAlister house on Wild Rose Lane?"

"The little brick bungalow? I always thought that place was so beautiful. It's a pity it's been abandoned for so many years."

"It's not abandoned any more." Ben smiled. "I'm fixing it up. The place has fantastic woodwork, but it's been quite a project getting it brought into the twenty-first century."

"I've always wondered what that place looked like inside. You're not making it too modern, are you?"

"Why would I do a thing like that? No, I'm putting in new appliances and ductwork, but keeping the classic style with the woodwork and the wood-beamed ceiling. Want to take a look?"

"I'd love to." Ginny blurted out her response before she considered the implications. She wasn't supposed to spend more time with Ben. But his description of the old house intrigued her. It would just have to be okay.

When they arrived, Ben took Ginny on a slow tour of the place, pausing several times when Ginny insisted he catch his breath.

"I'm not that weak. A little easy exercise is good for me," he defended himself when she all but pushed him into a chair.

"I don't care. It's my fault you were shot and I won't have you pushing yourself too hard." Besides making Ben rest, Ginny needed a good excuse for keeping him from hovering too close while she took her time looking at his bungalow. If she hadn't already had feelings for Ben, she might have fallen for him just on the basis of the work he'd done on the house. Care and craftsmanship were visible everywhere.

"I really love what you've done with the place," Ginny admitted as he led her toward the back door.

"Thanks. This place means a lot to me. And I've got the best view in the world." He led her out to the back, which looked out over the rolling hills. Half a mile away she could see the wrought-iron gates of the country cemetery where her father had been buried.

Ginny ambled along beside Ben, walking at a slow, leisurely pace, chatting about his house. She hardly realized how far they'd gone until they arrived at the cemetery. Her heart felt hesitant as they neared the row of tombstones where her father was buried.

She wasn't sure if Ben led the way or if her own feet brought her to a stop in front of her father's grave.

Henry "Cutch" McCutcheon III.

They stood in silence while a wren trilled its song from the wild roses that curled around the nearest stretch of fence. Ginny felt an involuntary sniffle escape, and Ben's arm met her shoulder. "I'm sorry." His bass voice rumbled with sympathy.

"So am I." Ginny sighed. "I should have been here for him. I should have been stronger."

"What do you mean? I thought you came home to visit and helped out with your dad pretty regularly throughout his illness."

"True." Ginny stared at the cold granite that marked her father's resting place. "Dad was first diagnosed with cancer when I was in high school. I tried to help, to drive him up to his appointments and back, since he wasn't supposed to drive himself and Mom was still working full-time then. I tried to be supportive of Mom, too, but I know a lot of the pressure of taking care of him fell to her. Still, I just couldn't take it. When I graduated, I left town. I ran off and joined the Dare Divas."

"Don't blame yourself." Ben pulled her tighter against him, and Ginny felt the pain in her heart subside a little, as it always seemed to do when Ben was there for her. "Cancer is tough on anybody. When you're a teenager and your dad is sick, it's more than anybody can expect you to handle."

"I should have handled it better than I did. I even thought about coming home to stay a few times, but after a week or two of taking care of my dad, I always went back to flying." Ginny looked past Ben's strong arm to where her father's name was carved into the stone.

McCutcheon.

She'd thought it was a weak name. A name that said cancer and illness and chemotherapy. By the time she'd left home, she'd resented it.

"You asked why I took the McAlister name to fly." She looked into Ben's warm green-brown eyes. "Everything I knew about the McAlisters was that they were strong and fearless pilots. And everything I knew about McCutcheons—" her throat swelled "—wasn't."

"So you wanted to be a McAlister?"

"I wanted to be brave. A fighter. Like you." As much as Ginny would have loved to stand there on the serene hillside in Ben's arms forever, she knew she didn't belong there. McAlisters were brave, but she wasn't a McAlister. Not really.

"You are brave." His face held a hope she knew she didn't deserve.

"No." She needed to leave. This was Ben's backyard. She'd already brought the killer too close. "I'm sorry, Ben." She pulled away from him. "I need to get going."

THIRTEEN

Ginny hardly had a chance to look at herself in the mirror, although when she did catch a glimpse, she liked the result. Elise's friend Kayla had done an amazing job on her hair, and the stunning periwinkle gown fit her to perfection, matching her eyes. She couldn't help but wonder if Ben would like the look, even though she chided herself for wondering.

Fortunately, the bridesmaids were too busy to give Ginny too much time to think. By the time everyone was finished getting their hair set and all the final touches on their makeup, it was time for pictures. And as if Ginny didn't have enough on her mind, Elise wasn't feeling well.

"Just a little upset stomach." Elise giggled and clutched her tummy. "You know, nerves."

"What do you have to be nervous about?" Phoebe Scarth, Elise's matron of honor, chided her friend. "Your real wedding was months ago. This day is for you to enjoy yourself. So enjoy yourself already!"

Ginny tried to take Phoebe's advice to heart, even if her words were intended for Elise. But her stomach was in knots just thinking about seeing Ben again, and walking down the aisle with him. "My tummy feels a little upset, too," she confessed to Elise. "Do you think I might have the same thing you do? Maybe it was something we ate at the rehearsal dinner last night."

"Oh, no!" Elise assured Ginny with an emphatic shake of her head, "I don't think we have the same thing."

"Okay." Ginny didn't know how Elise could be so sure, but she had to admit she was probably right. Though she'd have liked an excuse to think otherwise, she knew her stomach troubles had more to do with a certain handsome McAlister than with anything she'd eaten.

Fortunately, Phoebe found a packet of peppermints in her purse and passed them around to settle everyone's stomachs, and then they proceeded from the church parlor to the sanctuary for pictures. Ginny spotted Ben standing in line to have his boutonniere pinned to his tuxedo jacket, and her heart began doing an excited dance. If her heart had arms, she was sure it would have been pointing at Ben saying *there he is!*

As it was, she found herself looking at him, and when he turned her way, she grinned giddily in spite of herself. She gave him a friendly wave and tried to look casual as she walked over to join him.

"How are you doing?"

"I'm feeling better, but—" he twirled the boutonniere by its stem between his fingers "—I think I might need help with this."

Ginny couldn't help smiling at how adorable the strong military man looked, thwarted by an innocent flower. "I wouldn't want you to stab yourself," she teased him. "You can't afford to lose any more blood."

They giggled as she pinned the flower in place.

"Ginny!" Phoebe's voice behind her drew her attention. "Bridesmaid picture. Come on." Phoebe sounded impatient and, as Ginny caught up to her, she shook her head. "How many times do I have to say your name?"

"Once?"

"That was at least five," Phoebe laughed, "but nice try."

While Ginny did her best to follow the photographer's instructions on where to stand and when to sit, her mind buzzed with thoughts of Ben. It didn't help that she kept catching glimpses of him through the crowd, or hearing his booming laughter echoing over the chattering wedding party.

She needed to stay focused, not just for Cutch and Elise's sake, but because trouble, as it had been known for the past few weeks at least, could strike at any time. And whoever had attacked Ben had been lying low ever since. Which made Ginny suspect they might be plotting something. Something big.

Ben found Tyler hanging out with the other ushers near the front of the church. "Hey, little brother," he greeted him. He still hadn't figured out why Tyler had been appointed an usher while Ben got to be a groomsman, but if it meant he got to walk in with Ginny, he wasn't about to complain. Far from it.

"Ben!" Tyler hurried over to meet his brother, away from the other ushers.

"What's up?"

"Ginny learned Earl Conklin's alias. I looked him up. He's Allen Adolph, Doug Adolph's son. He's got a record a mile long."

Ben's heart froze at his brother's words. "He fits the stats of the man who shot me. Right size. His voice—" Ben pinched his eyes shut, remembering the angrily shouted words. "Even his voice fits. What do you think?"

"I don't know what to think. The man has been more than helpful with every stage of my investigation."

"Perhaps to divert suspicion away from himself?" Ben posed. "After all, if he can keep you busy investigating other people—"

"It leaves me less time to investigate him," Tyler finished for his brother, his expression grim as the man's possible intentions sunk in.

"Does Allen Adolph have a motive?"

"Maybe he's working for his father," Tyler suggested.

Ben grimaced at the suggestion. "I sure hope not. Ginny adores Doug Adolph and he dotes on her. She even told me he's like a second father to her. After losing her own father, it would tear her apart to know Doug was the one after her the whole time."

"I've got a few calls out to Wyoming right now, trying to determine if Earl Conklin has solid alibis for the times of the previous incidents. I'll run home and check my messages before the reception. The deputies out there agree the man deserves looking into, but right now we don't have sufficient cause for a search warrant, and last I checked, they didn't even know where he was."

Ben's eyes narrowed. He didn't like the sound of things. "I think we need to learn everything we can about him, and quickly. Ask the deputies if they can learn anything more from the other Dare Divas pilots. There were a couple of girls—Veronica and Jasmine, I believe—who acted pretty willing to help with the deputies' investigation. Maybe they've witnessed something that can supply enough information for a search warrant."

"It seems like a stretch." Tyler made a face.

"But it may be all we have right now." Ben didn't budge. "If he's the guy, we've got to put him away. Every lead deserves pursuing."

"I'll give the deputies a call and see what they can work out."

Glad for his brother's help, Ben asked, "In the meantime, do you think I should tell Ginny our suspicions about Allen Adolph?"

Tyler shook his head. "We don't know anything yet. I don't think we should spook her for no reason. She's been under enough stress with everything that's happened. Let her enjoy her brother's wedding. But keep a close eye on her."

Ben smiled. "I intend to."

As the string quartet played "Canon in D," Ginny stepped forward and wrapped her right hand around Ben's steady arm. She was worried about how he'd do so soon after his injury, but his eyes twinkled and he looked good. He looked *great*.

Pulling her gaze away from his handsome face, she turned her attention to the front of the church and made every effort to walk without tripping, conscious that her ankle was particularly susceptible to re-injury so soon after healing. They reached the front without incident, and Ben bowed slightly as he freed her arm from his and went to take his place next to the other groomsmen.

Ginny found her spot, a perfect vantage point from which to sneak peeks at Ben. Not that she was looking. As the bridal march began and the congregation stood, Ginny turned her head to watch a glowing Elise enter on her father's arm. Bill McAlister beamed with pride, and for an instant, Ginny wondered what kind of stepfather he would be. Given how close he and her mother seemed to be, Ginny figured she might eventually find out.

Where was Tyler? Ben knew his brother had planned to step out and check his messages, and he supposed

Tyler might have some follow-up phone calls to make, but dinner was already being served and Ben saw no sign of the younger McAlister. He hoped nothing had happened to him.

Fortunately, Ginny was okay. Ben watched her from across the head table, where the bridesmaids sat at Elise's right, and the groomsmen stretched out to the left of Cutch. The ceremony had been beautiful and Ginny was radiant.

And now Tyler was going to miss the toasts.

Cutch stood and graciously thanked everyone for attending. Beaming with pride, he reminded everyone that he and Elise had actually been married many months before, and that they were pleased to make an announcement about their growing family.

Ben looked over at Ginny. He knew what was coming, but by the way Ginny watched her brother with her mouth hanging open, Ben realized she hadn't guessed their secret.

Elise stood proudly beside her husband. "We're expecting a baby in November."

Cheers erupted as people hooted and clapped for the beaming couple. Ginny looked over at Ben, the shock clear on her face. He chuckled and shrugged.

"You knew?" She mouthed her question to him.

Ben couldn't keep from grinning.

Ginny narrowed her eyes at him as though she was upset with him for not telling, but he knew she wasn't really angry. She was smiling too much.

Tyler still hadn't shown by the time the emcee announced the first dance. Ben was really beginning to worry about his brother. While the bride and groom shared their customary dance, Ben called his brother on his cell phone from the corner of the reception hall.

"Yeah?" Tyler answered, sounding distracted.

"Where are you?"

"On my way. I've got dirt on Conklin, or Allen Adolph, or whatever you want to call him."

"Dirt?"

"I'll tell you when I get there. I need both hands to drive."

"Stay safe." Ben closed the call just as the bridal party dance was announced. His eyes found Ginny where she milled outside the ladies room with the other bridesmaids. She looked surprised.

"I forgot about this part," she confessed as he stepped closer to claim her for the dance.

He wrapped an arm around her waist and pulled her onto the dance floor. "Why do you think I got better in such a hurry?" He pulled her close.

"You recovered from being shot so you could dance with me?" Ginny asked the question in a teasing voice, but her eyes looked misty.

"What choice did I have?" Ben met her eyes.

That was a mistake. His heart tugged inside him, and he closed his eyes. He couldn't look at her, couldn't think about all he was giving up by letting her go.

She wasn't his. A woman like Ginny needed open sky to fly in, and he wasn't about to ask her to let him cage her up or tie her down. Maybe, if he really thought she had feelings for him in return, he might have broached the issue. But other than a few still moments when the air between them had seemed charged with electricity, Ben had no proof that he was anything other than a sorta friend, sorta shoestring relative who might be lucky enough to get a card at Christmastime if Ginny was the type who bothered to send them.

Which Ben got a feeling she wasn't.

So he had to be okay with that.

"You knew—" Ginny's voice pulled him away from his thoughts "—about Cutch and Elise expecting a baby?"

"Guilty as charged." He smiled at her. "But I thought maybe you guessed it when Tyler made that comment about Cutch not letting Elise fly her own plane."

"*That's* why he didn't want her to fly?"

"Sure. It's not like he'd try to stop her otherwise. Elise isn't the kind of girl who takes very well to being told what to do. Cutch is smart enough to respect that."

As Ginny leaned a little closer to him, Ben held her close, and she tipped her cheek against his shoulder.

Ginny's mind swirled with conflicting thoughts. Cutch wasn't a controlling husband. That was a relief. Ben had been laughing, not because Cutch was controlling Elise, but because Ben knew Tyler had almost given away the secret her brother and his bride had wanted to announce at their wedding celebration.

So maybe Ben wasn't the controlling kind. Maybe he wasn't like Kevin, maybe…maybe it didn't matter anyway how wonderful Ben might be. Ginny struggled to remind herself of all that was at stake. It didn't matter, even if she and Ben would make the perfect couple.

He'd been shot because of her. Until the madman after her was behind bars, she needed to get away from Ben permanently. And she needed to get that fact through her head before she did anything stupid, like reach up and kiss him.

Because she really, really wanted to kiss him.

Ben reluctantly let Ginny go when the music ended. She excused herself to the restroom and he watched her hurry away, mindful that Tyler had warned him to keep an eye on her.

As though he'd known his big brother was thinking about him, Tyler finally entered the room, made eye contact with Ben and trotted toward him.

"Where's Ginny?"

"Restroom."

"Okay. She should be safe in there." Tyler caught his breath.

"How bad is it?" Ben asked.

"Bad." Tyler shook his head. "The pieces have been falling into place fast. When I talked to the deputies to give them your tip about talking to Veronica and Jasmine, they'd already done some digging in their records. Turns out, Earl Conklin, aka Allen Adolph, visited Bobby Burbank right after he was arrested. He claimed that he wanted to ask the man some more questions. He was the last person to see Bobby Burbank alive."

"No." Ben winced, thinking of how close he'd let Allen Adolph get to Ginny. He'd sat in her trailer while "Earl" interviewed her—the day before her trailer had been burned to the ground.

"It gets worse," Tyler continued. "The deputies had been in contact with Jasmine and Veronica. The girls did some poking around in Earl Conklin's office. There they found a file with clippings of every article following Kristy's accident, along with the press releases Doug had sent out to let the world know what had happened and to keep people posted on her condition."

"I suppose that makes sense…" Ben began.

"*And*," his brother continued, "they found drafts of press releases announcing another accident."

Ben swallowed.

"An accident involving Ginger McAlister."

"Ginny," Ben whispered, looking to the restroom door in time to see her exiting in the company of other women, chatting. She was fine for now, but Ben wasn't about to let her out of his sight.

Tyler quickly summed up the rest of what he'd learned. "When the girls testified to what they'd seen, the deputies got a search warrant to go through Earl's files. They just got back to me on what they found. There were letters Allen had written to his father over the years, asking to be allowed to fly in the air shows. Apparently Allen is a stunt pilot himself. He wanted to head up the team instead of Ginny, but his father thought the Dare Divas were more distinctive and therefore more profitable with an all-female fleet."

"So Allen was jealous of Ginny." Ben watched while several men joined the chatting group of women. He couldn't see everyone's face, but he could still see Ginny. She looked like she was enjoying herself, and he felt glad for that. She deserved to be able to have fun for once. "I suppose it didn't help that Allen's father, Doug, treated Ginny like a daughter, and put her face on all their ads and posters."

"Speaking of posters, they found a few posters of Ginger McAlister crumpled up in Allen's trash can. He'd apparently been using them on his dart board for target practice."

Ben looked his brother in the eye for a few seconds. He couldn't stand that someone would do that to Ginny—or to her posters, which he considered a fine work of art by virtue of their subject matter. When he glanced back over to check on Ginny, she was gone.

Air. She just needed air, and space and a clear head. Otherwise she was bound to go running back to Ben and confess how she really felt.

Excusing herself, she made it almost to the door before she all but bumped into a familiar figure.

"Earl!" She smiled up at the man who'd done so much to protect her. "What are you doing here?"

"Doug said I might find you here. He told me you were planning to come home once you'd made an appearance at the reception. I saw you dance. Now you're free to head home."

Home. The word sounded jarring coming from Earl, or Allen—but she wasn't about to explain how she knew his real name. He was right. She'd said she'd leave, and it was time. She glanced over her shoulder and saw Ben through the crowd, talking to Tyler.

It was more than time.

"How thoughtful of you." She glanced around as she spoke, looking for Cutch and Elise. Now where had they gone? "Just give me a moment to tell my brother good-bye."

"Perhaps it would be simpler to call once you get to Wyoming. With everything else he has on his mind, I'm sure he won't notice you're gone."

Recalling all the trouble her brother had gone to in sending Ben to bring her back to Iowa, Ginny figured Earl had a good point. If she told her brother she was leaving, he might try to make her stay. He might enlist Ben to help him. And she knew she wouldn't be able to leave if it came to that.

"Great idea," she chirped, realizing Ben and Tyler had taken steps forward through the crowd. She grabbed Earl's arm and pulled him through the door. "Let's get moving."

Ben pulled Tyler toward the spot where he'd last seen Ginny. "I don't see Ginny anymore. Come on, we've got to find her and warn her about Allen."

By the time Ben and Tyler made their way through the thick crowd enjoying the reception, most of the ladies Ginny had been chatting with had dispersed. But Ben spotted Megan walking by with a sticky-faced Noah en route to the restroom.

"Have you seen Ginny?" he asked.

"Sure." Megan smiled brightly at Ben while making an obvious point to turn her back on Tyler. "She was headed toward the parking lot."

"Parking lot?" Ben repeated, alarmed. "Was she alone?"

"Don't worry—" Megan wrestled Noah's sticky fingers away from her face "—she's perfectly safe. She was with Earl."

"Earl Conklin?" Ben asked, his heart plunging.

"Yup. The one and only." Megan stepped past him. "Sorry, I have to get this little guy cleaned up."

Ben didn't have to tell his brother to follow him. Both McAlister brothers darted through the crowd to the parking lot.

There they saw a few of their cousins catching a breath of fresh air.

"Have you seen Ginny McCutcheon?" Ben looked around frantically but caught no sight of her. She and Allen already had too much of a head start.

"She left with a big guy." One of the young ladies pointed to a vehicle topping the hill that led away from the reception hall. "That's them in that red car. They looked like they were in a hurry."

"Thanks." Ben looked at Tyler. "Where are you parked?" Ben had arrived at the reception hall in a carriage along with the rest of the wedding party. He had no wheels of his own.

"My Jeep's over here." Tyler pulled his keys from his pocket. "We'd better hurry."

* * *

Ginny glanced at the way Allen Adolph gripped the steering wheel. Was it her imagination, or was he in a hurry? Oh well, she told herself. She should be grateful. The sooner she got back to Wyoming, the sooner her loved ones would be safe. She was just glad Allen had shown up and offered to fly back with her that night. It was so sweet of Doug to send the security man. She wouldn't have felt safe making the long flight on her own. Not with all that had happened to her already.

They arrived at the airfield and Ginny hopped out, leading the way to her yellow wing-walker. She felt grateful to Ben and his father, Leroy, for overseeing the repairs. Now the sunny little bird was as good as ever, and ready for the long flight back to Wyoming.

"Safety is important," Allen announced, as Ginny prepared for the pre-flight check. "I'm going to look over every part of the plane, including the engine. We can't be too careful."

Ginny appreciated his thoroughness. "I might run home and change clothes while you take care of that." She looked down at her formal gown.

Allen frowned. "You fly in crazy outfits for all your shows. Why take the time to change? Besides, I don't think you should go anywhere alone."

"You're probably right." Since Ginny wanted to get out of Holyoake as quickly as possible, she appreciated the security man's sensibility. While she ran through the checklist inside the cockpit, Allen took care of everything outside the plane. In no time they'd both finished, and Allen crept past her to the backseat, donning the other headset so the two of them could communicate.

With her radio-equipped helmet in place, Ginny started

the plane and taxied for the runway, saying a silent prayer inside her head. *Lord, get me home safely.*

While Tyler navigated through the congested parking lot, Ben pulled out his cell phone and tried to reach Ginny. "Come on, Ginny. Pick up," he whispered.

"I don't think she had her cell phone with her." Tyler paused for the third time to let high-heeled celebrants pick their way past him to the reception hall. "It's not like she had pockets in that dress."

Ben thought about how amazing Ginny had looked in her bridesmaid gown. Nope, no room for pockets in that thing. He closed the phone with a disgusted groan. "Can't we get out of here any faster?"

"Not without running over someone." Tyler paused again as a slow-strolling couple passed in front of them through the lot. "Don't worry, bro. We'll catch up to her. How far away can she possibly get?"

Ben looked down the road where the red car had disappeared into the horizon. Even the dust cloud had settled back onto the gravel roadway. "Far. That road leads to the airfield."

As Tyler steered the Jeep onto the road, Ben's eyes scanned the horizon. How much of a head start had Allen and Ginny gotten? And what were Allen's plans?

"What did the press releases say?" Ben quizzed his little brother. "How was Allen planning to kill Ginny?"

"There were a couple based on the gunshots—that would be those close calls she experienced back in Wyoming, which of course Allen wrote off as stray hunting shots when they were investigated. Then there was the fire in her trailer, which was fortunately thwarted thanks to you." Tyler shifted the Jeep into fifth, topping the hills at a faster speed than Ben usually chose to drive on the gravel surface.

But he didn't care as much for his safety as he did about getting to Ginny. "So what do you think he has planned this time?"

"Plane accident." Tyler spoke without any uncertainty in his voice. "All the other articles were about plane accidents—some of those scenarios were based on previous attempts which, thankfully, weren't successful, but the most recent drafts the investigators found described an accident involving Ginny in her wing-walker. The versions differed between Nebraska and Wyoming, but Allen listed the same 'supposed' cause each time."

"What's that?" Ben braced himself for the answer.

"Her plane ran out of gas before she reached her destination."

Ben's hands fisted voluntarily. "All he'd have to do is siphon her gas, and adjust her gauge to make her think she still has plenty to fly on." He shook his head forcefully. "We can't let her get on a plane."

But even as he spoke, Ben heard the blood-chilling drone of a small plane taking off. A moment later, Ginny's yellow stunt plane appeared over the tops of the trees.

"Too late." Tyler's voice sounded hollow as he gunned the Jeep forward with greater speed. "Looks like Allen Adolph is one step ahead of us."

FOURTEEN

Ben leaped out of the Jeep before Tyler had brought it to a complete stop. He raced inside the airstrip office, quickly climbing to the small windowed tower that held the radio. The injury under his ribs stabbed at him and he clutched at it, applying pressure to ease the pain as he switched on the radio.

He tried the airstrip's frequency first, hoping Ginny might still have her radio set for air-to-ground communication. "Big Ben to Firefly, Big Ben to Firefly," he prompted frantically.

Tyler had followed him up the stairs and observed, "She must have switched it to air-to-air already. Allen probably has a headset on." He placed his hand on his brother's shoulder. "Take it easy, Ben. Deep breaths. You still haven't recovered from your injury. You don't want to open up your stitches."

"I don't care about my stitches." Ben switched the radio to 122.75, the frequency for air-to-air chatter.

"You won't do Ginny any good if you end up in the hospital."

Ben realized his brother had a point. If they'd interpreted Allen Adolph's plans correctly, he had no intention of ever letting Ginny back on the ground alive. Ben and Tyler were her only hope. If he passed out, she'd be done for.

"Do you still have the phone number for the sheriff's office back in Wyoming?"

"I programmed it into my phone."

"Good. Give them a call. Tell them what's up. They've got to have a warrant by now to arrest Earl Conklin or Allen Adolph or whatever you want to call him."

"They sure do."

Ben sucked in another breath and felt the pinch in his side ease slightly. "Have them get a federal team on it. I don't care who. I want her plane intercepted."

Tyler punched the buttons and headed back down the stairs.

Finally able to breathe again, Ben tried reaching Ginny's plane. "Big Ben to Firefly. Big Ben to Firefly."

The response was mostly static. "Ben?" At least that much was Ginny's voice. "—fly…leave…later." Her words were coming in spurts and sputters, with overwhelming stretches of interference in between. "Understand."

"Ginny! Ginny!"

Nothing but static.

Ben slammed his fist down on the table. She'd flown out of range already. His mind raced a lot faster than his feet as he eased himself down the stairs as quickly as he could without upsetting his injury.

He *had* to reach Ginny. But if Allen Adolph had a headset on, whatever message Ben gave Ginny would be overheard by the man who intended to kill her. Even if he managed to get in contact with her, how on earth was he supposed to warn her without spooking Allen into going through with his evil plan that much sooner?

"That's all I know," Tyler spoke into his phone. "I appreciate your help. Thanks." He closed the call and looked up at Ben. "They're trying to pull something together."

"Trying?" Ben shook his head. "She needs help now."

"Were you able to get in touch with her?"

"Barely. She's out of range. I got just enough to tell me she's in that plane." He moved toward the office door as quickly as he dared. "Come on."

"Where are we going?"

"Up." He looked his brother in the eye. "Do you think Allen has any intention of letting Ginny land that plane alive?"

Tyler grimaced. "I honestly doubt it. Those press releases were dated *tonight*."

Fear charged through Ben's veins, the adrenaline masking the pain from his injury. He stood a little straighter. "Then right now we're her only hope."

"I'll run ahead and prep a plane. You take it easy. I'll bring her around." Tyler sprinted off as he finished speaking.

Ben watched his brother with pride and gratitude welling in his heart. Then he eased his way out to the tarmac. Tyler was right. He had to take it easy. Already he felt lightheaded from all he'd done that day. And he was pretty sure things were going to get a lot harder before he had a chance to rest.

Tyler brought Elise's Cessna around just as Ben reached the start of the runway. He climbed aboard, donned his headset and Tyler gunned it for the air.

"Do we have a plan?" Tyler asked once he had the plane climbing in the sky.

"Get close enough that I can talk to her."

"Then what?"

Ben wished he had a better answer. "Somehow I have to

convince her to land without tipping Allen off to the fact that we're on to him."

Tyler made a face. "How do you think you're going to accomplish that?"

"I don't know."

The brothers flew in silence for a few more minutes before Tyler grinned broadly. "I've got an idea."

"Hurry up and tell me before we get within range of their plane. If Allen hears your plan, there's no way it will work."

"We've still got some time." Tyler dismissed Ben's concerns. "Here's my idea. We fly within range of Ginny's plane. You declare your love for her. Tell her—"

Ben couldn't let his little brother continue. "What? No. No way. Who says—"

"Don't try to tell me you're not in love with Ginny. We don't have time for your excuses."

Realizing his brother was right on both counts, Ben swallowed back his embarrassment at having been discovered.

Tyler continued. "It's your excuse for coming after her. See? If we fly up and say, 'Hey Ginny, Allen's out to kill you,' he'll knock her right out of the sky. But if you declare your love for her, well, it makes sense, doesn't it? Spurned lover, left behind—"

"I'm not a spurned lover. Ginny wants to live her own life without me. I have no intention of revealing my feelings to her."

"You don't have a choice." Tyler didn't look at his brother, but kept his eyes on his instruments. "We should be coming up on her plane shortly, assuming she's headed in a straight line back to Campbell County."

Ben shook his head regretfully, wishing they knew for

sure which way Ginny was headed. "We really should start making people file flight plans."

Tyler snorted at the suggestion. "If we did that, then everyone would have to file them—including us."

Ben knew his brother was right. Most small airfields didn't ask for people's flight plans. It was just paperwork and bother, and there was more than enough open sky for everyone. Still, a flight plan would have helped stall Ginny tonight.

"Have you thought of a better excuse?" Tyler's voice pulled him from his thoughts. "You'll endanger her even more if Allen suspects we're on to him."

Ben mulled over his brother's suggestion. He'd promised himself he'd let Ginny go without a fight. She valued her freedom. She deserved her freedom. But at the same time, he saw no other way around it. He had to have some excuse for flying after her, some excuse to ask her to land. What other option did he have?

"It's not like you'd be lying," Tyler reminded him, as though he'd guessed what his brother was wrestling over.

"I know. I just don't want to have to explain my real motive to her afterward."

"At least she'll still be alive to have that conversation."

Tyler's words confirmed what Ben knew. He had no other choice.

"Okay. Let's do it. But not another word about it over the headset. We could come into range of them any time."

From near the horizon behind them Ginny saw the plane approaching, but it wasn't close enough yet for her to make out any distinctive marks. "We're not alone in the sky."

"Oh my," whispered Allen Adolph, or Earl Conklin, as Ginny was supposed to still be calling him, having not yet confessed to the man that she was aware of his alias. "I hope it's not someone coming after you on purpose."

Ginny bit back a terrified yelp. How had her pursuer caught up to them so quickly? "Maybe that's what that transmission from Ben was all about. Maybe he was trying to warn me." Her voice broke off, and she focused on taking steady breaths. "I should have circled around to hear what he had to say."

"Then you'd just be that much closer to whoever it is that's coming after you."

"Good point." Ginny wished her little stunt plane was capable of flying faster, but it was built for maneuverability more than speed. Pretty much anything in the air could catch it, including whoever was coming up behind them. "Are they close enough for you to get a decent look at them?"

Allen had his head cranked around, peering through the narrow windows. "Looks like a single engine."

"Any chance they're headed somewhere else? Maybe it's just a coincidence that we're sharing airspace."

"They seem to be gaining on us." Allen's voice held disapproval. "If I had to guess, I'd say they were trying to catch up to us."

Memories of the dogfight over a different stretch of Nebraska sent shivers of fear chasing up Ginny's arms. She gripped her controls with sweaty palms, her mind racing. What if her stalker really had come after her? Had that been what Ben was trying to tell her? She'd caught a note of something—fear, maybe—in the few words that had carried through the static-filled transmission.

But if Ben knew someone was after her, wouldn't he try to stop them?

Unless he couldn't.

The image of Ben lying in his own blood at the airstrip

office filled Ginny's mind. He'd nearly died because of her already. What if he'd been attacked again? For a moment, she was tempted to turn the plane around.

"It looks like a Cessna." Allen had his face pressed against the window, looking back. "Don't some friends of yours fly a Cessna?"

"Yes." Ginny's voice wavered, thinking of Elise's Cessna that Tyler had flown out to rescue them over Nebraska. But how did Allen know about the plane?

"Big Ben to Firefly. Big Ben to Firefly. Do you read me?"

"Ben!" Ginny was far too shocked to bother with standard air-to-air communication protocol.

Allen seemed more than surprised—he sounded quite displeased. "Big Ben, what are you doing?"

"I need to talk to Ginny." Ben's request transmitted clearly. "Alone, please. Can you take off your headset?"

"No," Allen growled. "Anything you need to say to her, you can say to me."

When Ginny glanced at Allen, he explained, "For all we know, Ben might be the person who's been trying to kill you."

"That's ridiculous!" Ginny gasped, aware that Ben had surely heard Allen's accusation, since they were all on the same frequency.

"Is it? Your troubles have only gotten worse since Ben entered the picture."

But Ginny knew Allen's theory was unfounded. "Ben saved my life. Repeatedly." She decided it wasn't worth arguing about. "Ben, what did you want to tell me? You'll have to just ignore Allen. He's only concerned for my safety."

"I want you to come back to Holyoake."

"Why?" Ginny noticed that Allen sat up a little straighter at Ben's words.

"Because I love you, Ginny. I don't want you to leave."

"What?" Ginny's heart flip-flopped, and she had to focus on flying the plane. Ben loved her? "I didn't know. You never said anything."

"I didn't want to let on how I felt. You're so young and beautiful and talented, I know you deserve better than a guy like me. You belong in the sky, flying with your stunt troupe. I know you need to be free. But when you left me at the wedding, I realized I couldn't let you go without telling you how I feel. It's up to you whether you leave or go, but whatever you do, just know I love you."

Ginny's eyes filled with happy tears at Ben's confession. Could it even be possible? After all her prayers that God would work things out—she'd never really believed it would happen. But if Ben loved her, maybe God had been listening after all.

Maybe God had sent Ben to bring her home.

With sudden conviction, Ginny realized why it had sounded so wrong when Allen had referred to Wyoming as "home." It wasn't her home—not anymore. She belonged in Holyoake with the people she loved. With Ben.

She wanted to throw herself into his arms. But first she had to get on solid ground.

"Big Ben, this is Firefly. Stay clear. I'm coming around."

"What?" Allen gasped. "You can't be serious! We've got to get you back to Wyoming where it's safe."

"I'm clear, Firefly." Ben's voice met her ears. "Come around."

Ginny barely hesitated. Sure, Allen had an excellent point. If she went back to Holyoake, she'd put her loved ones in danger again. But now that she knew Ben was in love with her, nothing was going to stop her from throwing herself in his arms and finally kissing the man she loved. God had brought them this far. With a surge of hope, she realized God had already gone to great lengths to bring her home. She was ready to trust God to keep her safe.

"Coming around." She prepared to turn the plane. But before she made a move, Allen's hand gripped her wrist.

"Oh no, you don't."

Ginny looked up. Allen had torn his headset off, so Ben would have no idea what he was saying. "What are you doing?" She tried to wrestle control away from the larger man, but he was stronger than she was. "Why are you stopping me from turning around?"

"I'm here to protect you, even if that means protecting you from yourself!" Allen's firm grip kept her from turning the plane.

"Is everything okay up there?" Ben's voice transmitted through the radio in her helmet.

"Al—er—*Earl* doesn't think I should turn back." Ginny had to remember that Allen Adolph didn't know she knew his real name. Until she had a chance to explain why she'd learned it, she didn't intend to let on about her knowledge, either.

"Firefly, this is Big Ben. You're clear to come around."

Ginny bit her lip. Allen's grip on her wrist was unrelenting. "Big Ben, this is Firefly." She wanted so much to run to him and tell him she loved him too, but she felt torn by Allen's insistence that she leave, and stymied by his unrelenting grip on her wrist. "I don't think I can."

FIFTEEN

Ben peeled back his headset and spoke directly into his brother's ear. "Get me on top of that plane."

To his credit, Tyler didn't question Ben's request. He'd heard the whole conversation with Ginny. He knew how desperate their situation was.

While Tyler got the plane in position, Ben pulled out an emergency parachute and strapped it on. He could only pray he wouldn't need it. He'd get one chance to do this right. If he missed, Ginny would be on her own.

Against Allen.

Which meant Ben *couldn't* miss.

Tyler covered his mouthpiece so his words wouldn't transmit to the other plane. "I'm almost in position. When I've got you as close as I'm going to get you, I'll give you this hand signal. Then you drop."

Ben watched his brother slice through the air with his hand. Good.

It had been mere seconds since he'd last spoken to Ginny, but he knew she and Allen had to be wondering what he was up to. He had to initiate his plan before either of them got suspicious. If the yellow wing-walker below him were to shift position suddenly, he'd miss.

And he couldn't afford to miss.

When the door unlatched, air blasted in at his face. Ben watched his brother. The moment Tyler's hand sliced through the air, Ben stepped out of the door into the empty air.

In order to avoid the chopping blades of the propeller, Ben had positioned himself to land a little closer to the tail. The metal bird seemed to rise to meet him and he smacked into its body, quickly grabbing hold of the metal handles, infinitely glad they were there.

Then he used the rung-like grips to pull himself up the plane toward the door.

Both Ginny and Allen had to have realized what he'd done. The sound of two hundred pounds of solid airman hitting the plane would be difficult to miss inside that tiny cabin. Ben had a feeling Allen wouldn't be happy about Ben's sudden appearance, but at the very least, he'd distract him from harming Ginny.

Ignoring the pain to the wound in his gut, Ben crawled against the wind to the small door of the plane. Fortunately the wing-walker's rungs were positioned to enable climbing in and out of the door with relative ease.

Ben fought the wind and pulled the door open to find himself face-to-face with a sneering Allen Adolph.

"You're wasting your effort, Ben." The voice was the same as the person who'd attacked him at the hangar—the person who'd shot him.

As though recalling exactly where Ben would be weakest, Allen hurled his fist toward the spot under Ben's ribs where the bullet had torn through him.

Ben shifted his body sideways, narrowly missing the punch. Then he quickly pulled himself into the doorway.

Ginny was still flying the plane, but she looked more than a little distracted. "Ben!"

"Fly the plane!" Ben yelled as he attempted to wrestle past Allen into the safety of the small cabin.

Realizing he needed help, Ginny tipped the little bird at an angle, and both Ben and Allen fell inside against the far wall.

Ben groaned as pain shot through the wound in his side.

Allen was on his feet first, his fist raised to punch Ben in the face.

Instantly Ben had his hand up, blocking the blow and catching Allen by the wrist. As Ginny righted the plane, Ben rolled forward, pulling Allen down under him.

But the erstwhile security officer knew Ben's weakness, and brought his knee up under Ben's ribs.

Pain shot through his midsection, and with a scream, he lashed out at Allen, swiping his head with his open palm and sending him crashing face-first into the back of the pilot's seat.

Taking advantage of Allen's momentary daze, Ben pushed up, trying to stand. He made it as far as his knees before the other man lunged at him again.

Ben caught Allen by his arms, bracing himself against his attacker. The door, which had swung mostly shut when Ginny had tipped the plane at an angle, was still not latched. Allen seemed intent on shoving Ben back through the opening.

"What can I do to help you, Ben?" Ginny shouted from the controls.

"Keep me away from the door," Ben grunted, his struggle with Allen tearing at his injury.

This time, instead of a simple angled tip, Ginny sped to the left in a downward arc, sending both men reeling sideways into the back of her seat. And this time, Ben had the upper position.

"Don't help him!" Allen cried. "He's the one who's been trying to kill you."

Ben didn't bother to respond to the accusation, having finally gotten a decent grip on the man's shoulder with his left hand. He pulled back with his right and knocked him in the jaw.

As Ginny righted the plane, Ben stumbled back and Allen threw his weight forward, forcing Ben back toward the door, which swung open wider from the motion of the plane. Ben saw the evening sky keel toward him.

He tried to lunge back away from the opening, but he could feel that the wound in his side had opened up and he was losing blood again. Already his efforts were taking their toll. He wasn't sure how much longer he could fight.

Allen seemed to sense that he was gaining the upper hand. "I'll rid your life of this pest!" he cackled as he shoved Ben toward the door.

"No! Don't touch him!" Ginny shouted, abruptly tipping the plane back to the left, sending both Ben and Allen staggering away from the doorway again.

Allen regained his footing first and lunged toward Ben.

Ben reeled back, landing seated on the rear bench seat, and thrust his legs upward, catching Allen in the chest. He sent the man flying backward.

Ginny tipped the plane to the right, overcorrecting from the last dip, sending Allen's swaying form tottering toward the doorway.

Seeing his chance, Ben forced himself to his feet, tipping his teetering adversary toward the door. Allen wore a parachute—obviously in preparation for bailing out once the plane ran out of gas. Ben had already noticed Ginny wasn't wearing one. Ben didn't know how Allen had pulled off that trick, but the very thought that the man had been trying to kill Ginny made Ben furious.

His protective instincts raged against the man who'd threatened Ginny so many times, the man who'd very nearly managed to kill her already. With a mighty shove, he had Allen through the doorway, where his white-knuckled fingers caught the doorframe.

"Leave Ginny alone!"

"Never!" Allen screamed. He pulled himself forward, letting go of the doorway as he tried to tackle Ben once again.

With a slight—almost elegant—dip, Ginny tipped the plane to the right, and Allen Adolph fell through the open doorway into the night.

Panting, Ben staggered back, collapsing onto the rear bench seat, lightheaded from exertion and loss of blood.

"Ben?" Ginny screeched from the controls. "Are you okay?"

He wished he could tell her that he was.

Ginny wasn't sure what to do. She'd seen Allen Adolph's parachute open behind her, but the night sky was dark and in all the excitement, she wasn't even sure where they were anymore.

"Tyler, are you still out there?" Ginny spotted the Cessna in front of her as she tried to talk to Tyler over the headset.

"I'm right here, Firefly. You looking for a place to land?"

"Yes! And quickly. I think Ben passed out."

"Follow me." Tyler gave her instructions for a nearby airport, assuring her that he'd already contacted them moments before and requested they have a medical team waiting on the ground.

"And we need police or someone to go look for Allen," Ginny reminded him.

"Already on top of it," Tyler assured her. "Federal agents are on their way."

Ginny spotted the lights of the small Nebraska airstrip below her a few moments later and put down easily, bringing the plane to a halt and unbuckling her harness before springing to the back seat to check on Ben.

He groaned as she landed almost on top of him.

"Are you okay?" Ginny caught his face in her hands, kissing his forehead gently.

"I'll pull through," Ben assured her in a weak voice as the waiting medical team rushed the plane, pulling open the door and scrambling inside the small cabin.

Ginny pulled up the long skirt of her bridesmaid dress and stepped back, explaining as much as she knew of Ben's injuries as the team got to work helping him from the plane. He swayed as he reached the tarmac, and a medic shoved a gurney under him. The way he relented to being carted off, Ginny knew the tough guy had to be hurting. If his internal stitches had popped, which she figured was likely, the bleeding could be severe—even life-threatening.

While the paramedics shoved an oxygen mask over Ben's face and started an IV, Ginny turned to see Tyler land the Cessna before running over.

"Is he okay?"

Ben didn't raise his head, but lifted his free hand with a trembling "okay" sign.

As the medical team hoisted Ben into the back of the waiting ambulance, Ginny and Tyler followed, answering the paramedics' questions as best they could. Ginny kept her eyes on Ben's face to avoid looking at the horrible injury the medics had revealed when they'd peeled up Ben's tuxedo shirt.

"We're going to take him right in to surgery." One of the EMTs explained the next steps as they neared the hospital.

For the second time, Ginny watched Ben being rolled away through doors that barred her from following.

Fortunately, Tyler had plenty to tell her to keep her mind off her concerns for Ben. As he explained it, Allen Adolph had been the one behind the attempts on her life. According to Tyler, Allen had hoped another accident would raise the Dare Divas' profile, making him seem like a hero, while at the same time, removing the greatest obstacle to his father's affections: her.

"I had no idea." Ginny shook her head, realizing, now that the missing pieces had fallen into place, just how jealous Allen must have been of her success. "When I think of all the times Doug praised my skills right in front of his own son—no wonder Allen hated me! I hope they catch him."

"I'll call and see what I can find out." Tyler excused himself.

After he left, Ginny was alone with her thoughts. She prayed Allen would be caught and that Ben would come out of his surgery successfully. Before she knew it, Tyler was back with more news.

"The feds pulled Allen Adolph out of a tree near where we saw his chute open. He came down kicking and screaming for his lawyer."

"That's a relief." Ginny sighed.

"And they've taken Doug and Ron Adolph into custody."

"Why?"

"For aiding and abetting a criminal. According to Allen, Doug picked him up in the sand hills after we tossed that rope into his propeller. And Ron encouraged him to find a spot flying for the Dare Divas."

"But I thought Doug was at a conference in North Platte?" Ginny recalled the alibi distinctly. "And Ron, too."

"They were. But Allen called Doug shortly after Doug's speech, and Doug drove out to pick him up. Allen wasn't far from North Platte at that point. Who knows if Doug or Ron realized what Allen had been up to?"

Ginny wondered the same thing. How involved had Doug been in his son's attacks? Surely he had to have some level of awareness, especially if Ron had been encouraging him. At the very least, they'd have been obligated to tell investigators what they knew of Allen's suspicious activities. But as far as Ginny knew, neither Ron nor Doug had ever made a peep about anything that might have implicated Allen in any of the incidents.

Tyler must have been thinking about the same issue. "The investigators are going to have their hands full sorting out just how much Doug and Ron were really involved."

"But they won't be able to manage the Dare Divas from behind bars."

"They won't need to." Regret filled Tyler's words. "The investigation is too tied up with the Dare Divas fleet. Every plane that has been tampered with, every bullet hole, every scrap of paper in their offices will have to be investigated."

"So what will happen to the Dare Divas?" Ginny asked.

"For right now—" Tyler shook his head sadly "—my guess is you girls might be out of a job."

Tyler's phone rang again, and he glanced at the caller ID. "It's Mom and Dad." He excused himself to take the call.

Ginny sat alone in the waiting room, the fancy sandals she'd worn to the wedding dangling from her fingertips, her mind stewing. What would become of all her talented flying friends if the Dare Divas were shut down indefinitely? The state fair season was quickly approaching— their busiest season of the year. She knew a lot of the new girls had payments to make on their planes, as well as regular living expenses. While Ginny had plenty saved up from her endorsement deals over the years, the others couldn't afford to miss a season.

"Dear Lord," she prayed, fully confident that the God who'd rescued her—the God who'd brought her home— would have an answer for her friends as well.

She'd no more than finished her prayer when a familiar voice spoke her name. Surprised, she looked up to see her mother and Bill entering through the waiting-room doors.

"What are you guys doing here?"

Her mother looked nervous. "Tyler told his folks where you were."

Ginny didn't understand. "But Tyler knew Ben had gone into surgery. They don't need to drive out here."

"They didn't," Anita McCutcheon explained.

Now Ginny was really confused. "So why did you two come to see him?"

Bill explained in a hesitant voice. "We didn't come to see Ben."

"We came to see *you*," Anita finished. "I know what it's like to sit in a hospital waiting room." Empathy shimmered in the unshed tears in her eyes.

"Oh, Mom," Ginny rushed forward and enfolded her mother in a big hug. "I should have been there for you."

"No." Anita hugged her back. "You were where you needed to be. God was with me."

"But I feel so guilty about not being there—" Ginny protested.

Her mother shook her head. "Not another word. I feel bad you had to help as much as you did. It was too much to ask of you at that age."

Ginny looked up and noticed Bill standing awkwardly behind her mother. She reached a hand toward him.

"I, uh…" He took half a step back.

"Come be a part of this hug," Ginny told him.

He smiled gratefully and put an arm around both of them. "You don't mind?"

Emotion swelled in Ginny's throat. "You did such a great job giving Elise away today." She pushed back a tear. "I thought maybe you might consider doing that for me someday."

An enormous grin spread across Bill's face. "I'd be honored."

Together they sat in a cluster of chairs in the waiting room and Ginny updated them on everything that had happened. When the doctor entered the waiting room, Ginny rose to her feet and brushed out the wrinkles in her dress.

"He came through just fine," the doctor informed her, "just a few popped stitches. No sign of infection. He just needs to rest." The doctor gave her a meaningful look. "No wrestling people out of airplanes for at least six weeks. Got that?"

Ginny nodded. "Can I see him?"

"He's right this way."

Bill and Anita were holding hands, but they each waved at her with a free hand to go on without them.

The doctor led her down the short hallway to the recovery room where Ben lay, looking weary, but thankfully a lot less pale than he had the last time she'd visited him after surgery.

"Ben!" She hurried toward him, grateful to see him awake—and alive.

He turned a tired smile her way. "Told you I'd be okay." He reached for the button that raised the head of his bed slowly upward.

Hurrying toward him, she cupped his cheek with her hand. "I didn't get a chance to tell you earlier." She couldn't wait to finally speak the words she'd been holding back ever since his plane had caught up to hers in the sky. "I love you, too, Ben."

Instead of the smile she'd hoped to see, regret crossed Ben's features. "I hadn't intended to tell you that. Allen was in the plane with you—I needed an excuse for flying after you. It was all I could think of. I don't—" He closed his eyes and his face filled with pain. "I don't expect you to love me back."

Confused, Ginny shook her head. "You don't love me?"

Ben's eyes popped open. "Of course I love you. You're amazing. But you deserve better than a guy like me."

More confused than ever, Ginny narrowed her eyes. "Better? Ben, there isn't anybody better than you. You're the man I love. You make my heart not hurt anymore. God used you to bring me home."

An uncertain smile stole across his face. "You can't mean that. Ginny, you've got your whole life in front of you. Any man in the world would give his right arm to be with you."

"I don't want any man in the world. And you can keep your right arm. I love you, Ben. I have since somewhere in the middle of the sand hills, I think. I just couldn't say anything because I didn't want to endanger you."

"Ginny." Ben raised his bed a little higher and reached for her. "Don't worry about putting me in danger. I just want you to be happy."

She felt a mischievous grin creep onto her lips. "You want to make me happy?"

"Of course."

"Can I borrow your airfield?"

Now Ben looked confused.

Ginny rushed to explain. "The Dare Divas need a new headquarters. A lot of the girls own their own planes. Oh, and we need a manager." She smiled down at him. "You retired from the Air Force to help run the family airstrip, didn't you?"

"Yes." Ben sounded cautious, but he was starting to smile.

"Perfect!" Ginny grinned. "Because we need to start booking state fairs, like, yesterday."

Ben grabbed her hand and pulled her closer. "Whoa there. Before you start making too many plans, I think we need to set terms." He reached one hand behind her head, lacing his fingers through her hair, drawing her face nearer to his.

Ginny's heart, which had somewhere very recently given up all its painful pangs, leapt for joy inside her chest. "What terms?"

"I was thinking something along the lines of, to have and to hold from this day forward. Isn't that what the preacher said today?" Ben drew her lips closer to his.

"I think he also said—in sickness and in health, for as long as you both shall live." Ginny's mouth hovered blissfully close to Ben's.

"Sounds like good terms to me." Ben leaned forward the last half inch and claimed her in a kiss.

Ginny melted. She loved this man. Oh, wow, did she love this man.

Ben eased back with a sigh onto the pillow propped behind him. "I don't deserve you."

"Maybe I don't deserve you."

"I think you both deserve each other." Tyler surprised them both by calling out from the doorway. "So are you two engaged, or what?" He held out his open cell phone. "Everybody at Cutch and Elise's reception has been waiting to find out." He looked behind him at Bill and Anita, who had their phones held at the ready.

Ginny looked down at the man she loved, into his Junefield green-and-brown eyes—eyes that made her heart happy.

He seemed to see through to her very soul. "I love you, Ginny McCutcheon. Now, you want to make good on your claim to be a McAlister?"

She raised an eyebrow at his curious proposal.

His voice softened. "Will you marry me?"

"Yes!" She squealed and threw her arms happily around his neck.

"Did you hear that?" Tyler's voice echoed behind them as he spoke into the phone. "She said yes." He paused. "They don't look like they want to take questions right now." Tyler's voice faded as he stepped away. "They're too busy kissing."

* * * * *

Dear Reader,

The phrase "dead reckoning" refers to a navigational process that uses an original known position and the estimated speed and direction of travel to determine current location. What does that mean? It means we don't always know where we are, but if we can look back on where we've been and factor in where we're headed, that can help us determine where we are—and where we need to go from there.

In *Dead Reckoning,* Ginny is lost—not just lost in the Great American Desert, but also wandering in a spiritual wasteland of fear, on the run from God's love. Just as shepherds seek out their lost sheep, Ben was sent to find Ginny and bring her home again. In the end, Ginny not only comes home to Holyoake, but she finds herself at home again in God's love.

Have you ever been lost? Sometimes we get lost physically and don't know where on earth we are. Other times, like Ginny, we become adrift from our loved ones and the family of God. Just as Ginny finally finds the family she's been seeking—through the love of her mother and brother, and Ben's offer to make her a McAlister—we all have a loving Father in heaven who eagerly seeks to welcome us home into the family of God.

If you're feeling lost, maybe now is a good time to look back on where you've been and determine where you're going. Like Ginny and Ben, I pray that you'll trust God to lead you home!

In Him,
Rachelle McCalla

Questions for Discussion

1. Ginny flew under the name of McAlister because she thought more highly of the McAlister family and their skills as pilots than she did her own. Have you ever wished you were part of a different family?

2. The life-threatening situations she's been through have caused Ginny constant stress induced pain, but she still refuses to give up flying. Does her choice make sense to you? Do you ever make risky choices just to keep doing what you love? Why or why not?

3. Ben has put Ginny on a pedestal because of her skills and fame as an acrobatic flier. Have you ever viewed someone else through rose-colored glasses?

4. Ginny doesn't want to consider that any of the people she trusts could be behind the attempts on her life. Have you ever thought someone was above reproach just because you felt close to them? Do you think it's wise to trust people simply because they're familiar to you? What are the benefits and risks of trusting others?

5. When Ginny's plane and later her rental car encounter the same kind of mechanical problems that caused Kristy Keller's crash, Ginny is doubly disturbed because they remind her of Kristy's accident and the guilt she felt about it. Are there certain things in your own life that are extra frightening because of something you've experienced in the past? Or do you know anyone who feels this way?

6. Ben chooses not to tell Ginny about Bill and Anita, because he feels it's their place to share their news with Ginny. Do you think he made the right choice? What would you have done?

7. When Ginny sprains her ankle, Ben insists on carrying her, even though he is exhausted already. How is his behavior similar to that of the shepherd carrying the sheep in the stained-glass window at the hospital chapel? How is it similar to the way God treats us?

8. When Ben tries to stop Ginny from telling Megan how to find her, Ginny becomes that much more determined to tell Megan where she is. Have you ever rebelled against a person who you felt was trying to control you? Was that the right choice? What might Ginny have done differently? How do you plan to handle things the next time someone tries to tell you what to do?

9. Allen Adolph feels jealous of Ginny and the attention his father, Doug, shows her. How does Allen's jealousy lead to poor choices? How might Allen have dealt with his jealousy in a constructive manner?

10. Doug Adolph has turned a blind eye to the things Allen did that might have tipped off investigators sooner to the fact that Allen was behind the attacks on Ginny's life. Do you feel Doug has failed in his role as Allen's parent? At what point do you think this pattern began in their relationship?

11. Ginny feels guilty that she didn't do more to support her mother and father during her dad's long fight with

cancer. Do you agree that she could have done more? What might she have done differently?

12. When Ben's father talks to Ginny in the hospital chapel, she's unsure if he's angry with her. How do you think Leroy McAlister felt? How might you have behaved in that situation?

13. Ben joined the Air Force "to be a hero." Have you ever wanted to be a hero? Do you think Ben accomplished his goal? How and why?

14. By the end of the story, Ginny has decided to trust God and has started praying again. She gave up praying because God allowed her father to die, and nothing has changed in that respect. What change convinced Ginny that she could trust God after all? Have you ever felt similarly, or known someone who felt this way?

15. Do you believe Ben and Ginny make a realistic couple? Do you think their love will last? Why or why not?

INSPIRATIONAL

Inspirational romances to warm your heart & soul.

SUSPENSE

TITLES AVAILABLE NEXT MONTH

Available August 9, 2011

REQUEST YOUR FREE BOOKS!

2 FREE RIVETING INSPIRATIONAL NOVELS
PLUS 2 FREE MYSTERY GIFTS

Love Inspired®
SUSPENSE

YES! Please send me 2 FREE Love Inspired® Suspense novels and my 2 FREE mystery gifts (gifts are worth about $10). After receiving them, if I don't wish to receive any more books, I can return the shipping statement marked "cancel". If I don't cancel, I will receive 4 brand-new novels every month and be billed just $4.49 per book in the U.S. or $4.99 per book in Canada. That's a saving of at least 22% off the cover price. It's quite a bargain! Shipping and handling is just 50¢ per book in the U.S. and 75¢ per book in Canada.* I understand that accepting the 2 free books and gifts places me under no obligation to buy anything. I can always return a shipment and cancel at any time. Even if I never buy another book, the two free books and gifts are mine to keep forever.

123/323 IDN FEHR

Name   (PLEASE PRINT)

Address   Apt. #

City   State/Prov.   Zip/Postal Code

Signature (if under 18, a parent or guardian must sign)

Mail to the Reader Service:
IN U.S.A.: P.O. Box 1867, Buffalo, NY 14240-1867
IN CANADA: P.O. Box 609, Fort Erie, Ontario L2A 5X3

Not valid for current subscribers to Love Inspired Suspense books.

**Are you a subscriber to Love Inspired Suspense
and want to receive the larger-print edition?
Call 1-800-873-8635 or visit www.ReaderService.com.**

* Terms and prices subject to change without notice. Prices do not include applicable taxes. Sales tax applicable in N.Y. Canadian residents will be charged applicable taxes. Offer not valid in Quebec. This offer is limited to one order per household. All orders subject to credit approval. Credit or debit balances in a customer's account(s) may be offset by any other outstanding balance owed by or to the customer. Please allow 4 to 6 weeks for delivery. Offer available while quantities last.

Your Privacy—The Reader Service is committed to protecting your privacy. Our Privacy Policy is available online at www.ReaderService.com or upon request from the Reader Service.

We make a portion of our mailing list available to reputable third parties that offer products we believe may interest you. If you prefer that we not exchange your name with third parties, or if you wish to clarify or modify your communication preferences, please visit us at www.ReaderService.com/consumerchoice or write to us at Reader Service Preference Service, P.O. Box 9062, Buffalo, NY 14269. Include your complete name and address.

LISUS11B

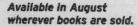